MUFASA

THE LION KING

MUFASA
THE LION KING

THE NOVELIZATION

Adapted by CHARLES ORGBON III

 PRESS

LOS ANGELES · NEW YORK

Printed in the United States of America
First Paperback Edition, December 2024
1 3 5 7 9 10 8 6 4 2
FAC-004510-24284

Library of Congress Control Number: 2023951246
ISBN 978-1-368-09931-8

Visit disneybooks.com

SUSTAINABLE FORESTRY INITIATIVE
Certified Sourcing
www.forests.org
SFI-01681

Logo Applies to Text Stock Only

To Gloria and Dalila
If only the world could love the way you do

CHAPTER 1: NOW

A storm brewed at the edge of the horizon, ready to roll across the savannah. The rising sun, which had seemed set to beat down and bake the clay soil, slowly disappeared, melting into a darkening glob.

A shoebill soared high in the sky over the Pride Lands, fighting against the wind that tried to slow his pace. His flattened bill and wide wings cut through the heavy air.

It won't be long now, he thought.

He landed on a ridge overlooking the disappearing sun, approximately half a mile from Pride Rock, ready to declare the entrance of the savannah's king for an important announcement. He puffed his chest, opened his bill, and started clapping it, each beat building upon the last until he created an intense resonance.

Only some creatures noticed the sound, which was familiar to them all, but no one joined in. Something was wrong.

The wind's powerful gusts picked up speed, carrying the scent of rain and dust. Its force cracked branches, and the grasses whined as they snapped back and forth.

The creatures scurried across the vast plain, searching for cover as the rumbling clouds barreled closer: Birds lunged into the sturdy branches of umbrella thorn acacia trees. Meerkats dove into their extensive networks of underground tunnels. Elephants huddled together in the open expanse, forming an unbreakable mass.

A young elephant calf slipped past his mother's warm embrace, wanting to feel the wind push against his face—but within seconds, she lowered her trunk to snatch him up with a tight squeeze.

A flash of lightning and a sharp crack of thunder echoed amid the increasingly darkening clouds, and the shoebill lost his concentration. He flinched and took flight into the wind. A deepening unease spread through the throng of animals as they shuffled in their places.

Then a roar, even more thunderous than the sky, echoed across the savannah.

The young elephant calf shivered and hid behind his mother.

"What's wrong?" the calf said, his voice shaking.

"It's the king. He needs us," she said.

The mother elephant nuzzled her young one, then raised her trunk to trumpet. Her powerful call echoed through the savannah, carried on the wind, and reached every corner of the land. The animals emerged from their burrows one by one, drawn by the urgent tone of her call, and responded with their own sounds: barking, grunting, snorting. They formed a motley herd and made their way through the raging storm, toward a clearing on the horizon.

In the center of the clearing stood a large rock, weathered and worn by centuries of use: Pride Rock. Here the community came together to celebrate, mourn, and make important announcements. The rock was a sacred place, a reminder that no matter what challenges they faced, they all belonged to the same family.

The animal kingdom knew their presence was needed. As the herd approached, animals of every size and shape filled the clearing, gathering together in anticipation of what was to come. The air was thick with the aroma of wet earth and foliage.

A lion walked out from the recess of Pride Rock: Simba, their king. His form was stiff and elongated, but his flattened ears and ever-roaming eyes hinted at his desperation. As he ended at the cliff, he bowed his head. Then he raised his head slowly and looked out into the crowd.

After a long sigh, he said, "My friends—Nala is missing. She ventured out to the northern border and was overtaken by the storm. I have looked everywhere, but now I need your help."

Their queen was missing! As the weight of the announcement settled in, the crowd fell into stunned silence.

"The storm is very powerful," King Simba continued. "I'm asking all of you to help me find her."

The elephant matriarch stepped forward and asked, "What about little Kiara?"

She motioned to Kiara, the sole child of Simba and Nala. Everyone adored her golden eyes and endlessly curious questions.

King Simba nodded once. "She's safe in the caves. I've called in the security detail."

One of the giraffes standing off to the side stepped up and asked, "Are you sure that's a good idea, Majesty?"

"I trust them," King Simba said firmly.

Heads turned, and the crowd broke out into murmurs. Before tension escalated further, a hyena spoke loudly over the crowd. "Enough! King Simba needs us. Storm or no storm—we must find the queen!"

As the animals dispersed to form search parties to

cover the entire northern border, King Simba looked toward the horizon. Quietly under his breath, with trembling words, he whispered, "Nala . . . where are you?"

ᐱᐯᐱᐯᐱ

As if King Simba's whisper could travel for miles, Nala looked up, thinking she had heard someone speaking to her. She pivoted only to find nothing behind her except for shrubs bending in the wind. She winced with every step.

Just ahead in the distance, Nala saw a rocky shelf. She sauntered underneath and growled at the little porcupine resting inside until it scurried away. She lay on the flat earth and slowly closed her eyes.

"Simba," she whispered. "I'm here. . . ."

She fell into a deep slumber, even with the clouds getting ready to rage for the next few hours.

ᐱᐯᐱᐯᐱ

The animal kingdom worked together to organize search parties. They divided the terrain into sections and split off to look for their queen. But tenacious meerkat Timon and loyal warthog Pumbaa followed a path opposite the search parties—straight to the cave at the top of Pride Rock, where Kiara rested. Simba had specifically called for them.

They turned down the rocky trail, Timon riding atop Pumbaa's back. Timon and Pumbaa had been friends for many years, and the warthog's wiry hair bristled against Timon's belly as they both whistled a jaunty tune.

They turned a corner and arrived at the entrance of the cave, but a pride of lions guarded the opening. Timon and Pumbaa found themselves staring into the lions' hardened eyes and froze, unable to decipher their next move.

"Security detail has arrived!" Pumbaa said, his voice rising in pitch as he fidgeted anxiously.

Timon wiggled. "Is everyone feeling more secure?"

All the lions offered blank stares.

Pumbaa stepped in closer. "I feel secure."

Still, the lions stood stoically.

Timon broke out into hesitant chuckles. "One gentle reminder," he began, waving his tiny paws back and forth. "We are not food."

Ignoring his growing nerves, Pumbaa added, "No. No. No. We are just two guys walking to work through a pride of hungry lions. . . ."

"Which is perfectly normal," Timon added. "I'm not terrified!"

"No," agreed Pumbaa, moving through the unmoving crowd of lions. "Whatever you're smelling, that's not fear, and it's also not the other thing you might be smelling from me."

King Simba awaited Timon and Pumbaa's arrival behind the pride of lions. The soft touch of the wind played with his golden mane, his presence commanding respect and admiration.

Timon stood straight, respectfully. "Security detail reporting for duty, Your Grace—Your Highness—"

"Ruler of all four-legged creatures." Pumbaa gestured to himself with a hoof.

"And that one three-legged zebra," Timon interjected.

"Oh, right, Ron," said Pumbaa. "That was tragic."

"It was an eat-and-run," joked Timon. He tried to hold back the series of giggles threatening to burst through his wiggling mouth.

"Yeah . . ." said Pumbaa.

King Simba rolled his eyes, but Timon did not stop. "Ron has three legs. That's still one more than me."

Pumbaa replied, "Well, are those arms or legs?"

"I don't know," said Timon. "I think they're paws."

"I consider all of those legs," Pumbaa said.

"Guys!" yelled Simba, commanding their attention. Pumbaa and Timon assumed their respectful poses. "This is serious. Nala is missing. We're going back out to find her."

"How can we help?" the two friends asked together.

"I need you to stay with Kiara until we come back," said Simba.

"Are you saying your security detail has been called to do babysitting?" asked Pumbaa. "'Cause that is perfect. I love babysitting. Can we stay up late? Can we have snacks? Where's the snack drawer? What's our bedtime? Can we build a fort? *Can we build a fort?*"

Timon kept his attention on King Simba but responded, "Pumbaa, we should really discuss this, because I don't really love children."

Simba sighed in exasperation. "Guys, I promised her everything would be okay."

Timon said, "Well, that's *one* way to parent."

"She's gonna have to grow up sometime," Pumbaa suggested.

Timon snapped, "What else did you tell her—that she can be whatever she wants to be?"

"That life is fair?" Pumbaa interjected, chuckling.

Simba drove his paw into the earth, sending a small vibration through the ground. Pumbaa and Timon became quiet and looked up.

"I need you to try and act normal," said the lion. "And most of all—no stories. Promise me."

"No stories . . ." said Pumbaa.

"Wait a second—" added Timon.

"Promise me!" King Simba interrupted.

Pumbaa gave up easily. "Okay, you know what, fine. No stories."

Simba turned away from them and entered the cave to lead them toward Kiara. First Pumbaa and Timon followed; then the rest of the lions carried the tail end.

"Speak for yourself, Pumbaa," Timon said, never the one to back down.

"No, shhh," said Pumbaa. "No stories."

Timon dropped his voice to a whisper. "Okay, as long as we can tell a story anyway. Okay, we'll tell him that we're not gonna tell a story, then we're gonna tell a story."

"He can't stop us," Pumbaa whispered back.

Simba looked over his shoulder. "You know I can hear you, right?"

At last they reached where little Kiara sat. King Simba did the hardest thing he had ever done: he said goodbye to Kiara. He nuzzled her and whispered, "Be brave now, Kiara. Be brave."

And then he left with the rest of his entourage as they paraded back out the way they'd come. When he'd breached the cave's entrance, King Simba released a powerful roar into the dark clouds, putting the strength of the thunder to shame. Then he and the lions started running, roaring, into the distance.

Silence hung in the damp air back inside the cave, where only Pumbaa, Timon, and Kiara remained. Timon, wanting to comfort the teary-eyed Kiara, blurted out, "Okay . . . who wants a story?"

Before anyone could answer, he dove into an engaging story of how he and Pumbaa had stopped a new false king named Scar from taking over Pride Rock.

"Scar looked at us—he knew it was the end of the line," said Timon. "I could smell the fear."

"That was actually me," said Pumbaa.

Timon described how he and Pumbaa fought Scar and pushed him over the side of Pride Rock.

"And then," Pumbaa concluded, "we ate him."

Kiara had paid careful attention to the story, and she

innocently asked, "So, you two defeated Scar? And then ate him?"

Timon smiled brightly. "Honestly, one of the best meals I ever had."

Kiara hummed a little before saying, "My dad told me *he* defeated Scar."

"Well, okay . . . but your dad, as we all know, is a pathological liar," Timon said.

"He's always lyin'," Pumbaa joked. "Get it?"

Lightning struck in the distance, and the trio jumped in fright. A roar of thunder followed, and Kiara darted behind a large boulder for refuge. Timon and Pumbaa followed her, huddling close and seeking comfort and safety in each other's embrace.

"I'm scared," said Kiara, her voice filled with trepidation. "I want Mom and Dad."

"Look, look, look, don't be scared, Kiara," said Pumbaa. "How about we sing you a song? And a one, and a two—"

"Pumbaa, no!" said Timon. "It's way too early for that song."

"It worked on Simba. He thought he had murdered his own father," Pumbaa began. "He was singing and dancing around in seconds!"

"I can't just turn it on like that," Timon said, a mix of disbelief and amusement etched on his face. "I have to be in the moment."

"He sang that song for six years straight," said Pumbaa.

As they huddled together, another bolt of lightning illuminated the area, revealing a mysterious silhouette. The shadowy figure stood on three legs, and the trio watched in awe and fear as it moved closer to them. The fur on the back of Kiara's neck stood on end as she tried to discern the strange newcomer's identity.

Timon shrieked, "It's Ron, the three-legged zebra! Run for your lives!"

Pumbaa screamed. "He heard what we've been saying about him." Then, almost pleading, he said, "We're sorry, Ron, they were jokes. They were just jokes!"

But Kiara squealed happily as her eyes filled with tears. "It's Rafiki! Rafiki!"

Rafiki ambled forward with a wooden walking stick, and Kiara rushed into his arms. He cradled Kiara's head and said, "Little one, there's no reason to cry."

She purred in his embrace. "My parents—they're gone."

Rafiki sighed. "Look out there, *mdogo*. You see those baobab trees blowing in the wind—how they bend but do not break. The roots of those trees are very strong, like your family. They go down into the earth. And even when you can't see them, they're all around keeping you safe."

"Man, he's good," muttered Pumbaa as he and Timon watched from the shadows.

"Yet it makes sense that he lives alone," said Timon.

Pumbaa was still in awe. "He's such a visual story-teller!"

Kiara's breathing evened out. "I just want the storm to pass. And then I promise to be brave!"

"I will tell you a secret," Rafiki said. "When Simba

was your age, he was afraid of the thunder—would hide behind the king."

Kiara leaned in even closer. "When did he stop hiding?"

Rafiki rested against one of the walls of the cave. "One day, during a big storm, Mufasa walked Simba to the very top of Pride Rock, told him to stand with him and howl into the wind. Simba slowly stepped out with the king—and together they roared into the night."

Kiara responded, "But I am not brave like my dad. And I could never be like Mufasa."

"Is that so?" Rafiki said with an arch of his brow. "Then maybe it's time I tell you a story—a story of a cub not much bigger than you, a lion born without a drop of nobility in his blood. A lion who would change our lives forever."

Pumbaa and Timon emerged from the shadows, Timon riding atop Pumbaa's back with a tray of wriggling treats in his hands.

"A story!" said Pumbaa. "I'm so glad I brought some crickets!"

As Timon dismounted, Pumbaa popped a bug in his mouth.

"Go easy," said Timon. "We're in a cave."

Rafiki led Kiara to the edge of the plinth of Pride Rock. Kiara looked down at Rafiki's lowered palm, which now held dust and rock.

"This story begins far beyond the mountains and the shadows—on the other side of the light," he said. "In this place, everything was dying of thirst—as twenty full moons had passed without a single drop of water. But when the skies finally opened, destiny would reign. . . ."

He blew the dust and rock into the expanse of the cave, and as it swirled, Kiara could almost envision the story unfolding before her eyes.

CHAPTER 2: BEFORE

The parched plains simmered cruelly, demanding more and more from the animals that struggled to survive in its harsh embrace.

A mother giraffe scavenged for remnants among a dying marula tree's high branches, until she found one single leaf hanging like a precious jewel. The leaf made a crunching sound as she clamped on it. She passed it to her calf, who eagerly devoured the leaf, his first meal of the already long day.

Dark clouds rushed in from the west, and the once bright and sunny day transformed into a rainy one. The animals scurried restlessly, seeking shelter from the impending storm.

The young giraffe's ears perked up in anticipation. As he gazed at the turbulent sky, he sensed that something was about to change. The first drops of rain fell, splattering against the dry ground with a hollow thud.

Half a mile away, a lion named Afia limped out from under the shade of a dead baobab tree. Her legs barely held the weight of her body.

She tilted her head back to observe thick, dark clouds that stretched out like fingers across the sky. A subtle but palpable sense of relief washed over her. The approaching storm held the promise of a fresh start: a cleansing of the past and a chance for new beginnings. The rain would bring new life to the savannah, the grass would once again turn green, and the animals would thrive. She had seen it happen before and knew it would happen again. The drought would soon be over.

"Look!" Afia said to her partner. "Do you see . . ."

Masego moved up beside her, his body as weak as hers

from the drought. The two lions glanced at each other with hope in their eyes.

"I see it," Masego said, his voice choking.

Tiny little droplets of water started dancing down from the sky and quickly vanished as the earth gobbled the bits of moisture.

"Mufasa! Mufasa! *Come see!*"

A small cub appeared from the rocky den located behind Afia and Masego. He looked around, smiled, and bounced down to them. A fat drop of rain hit Mufasa square on the head, and he burst into happy giggles.

"Rain, rain! Finally, we have rain!" Afia proclaimed.

Masego and Afia scurried toward the hilltop, Mufasa right at their heels. They stood at the edge of the hill, looking out as the rain puddled around their feet.

"Mom—what is that light way out there?" asked Mufasa. He turned his head pointedly toward the south, where the lightning struck the ground every couple of seconds.

Afia followed his gaze. "Oh, that's very special. Beyond

the horizon, beyond the last cloud in the sky. That's a place we call Milele."

"Milele?" Mufasa asked with a tilt of his head.

"It means 'forever,'" Afia said.

"Imagine a kingdom full of life, water, and food," Masego added. "Grass and sky as far as the eye can see."

"Will we ever go there?" Mufasa asked.

Afia ran her nose along her cub's ears. "Oh, we can right now, Mufasa. We can close our eyes—let our dreams take us."

Mufasa closed his eyes and allowed the sensation to wash over him as the coolness of the rainwater refreshed his skin and weighed down his fur.

While the family stood on the ridge, a watering hole quickly grew below, and visitors began to arrive: elephants, giraffes, zebras, birds, monkeys. Electric happiness moved through them all, young and old. The watering hole grew larger and larger, like a bowl being filled by a pitcher, creating an oasis.

As the water level rose, the animals' spirits also lifted.

Soon the entire group could take turns drinking and cooling off. Afia felt a surge of joy within her and began to sing a happy tune, imagining Milele. Perhaps what she was witnessing could become its own version of Milele, a place where the water always flowed and the savannah teemed with vibrant life.

Amid the rainy landscape, a slender ray of light beamed onto the savannah floor.

Mufasa looked at Masego and squinted happily. "Dad, race you to the light!"

Masego smiled at his son's sparkling eyes. Maintaining his perch at the edge of the hilltop, he said, "You're too fast. I've never beaten you! Nobody has ever beaten you!"

"I know!" Mufasa said righteously. Before Masego could react, Mufasa bolted, running down the craggy slope.

Masego appreciated his son's leaping form. "Ahhh . . . the fastest cub in the world!"

Afia and Masego watched their son approach the watering hole, fearless in the thunder.

"Maybe we shouldn't fill his head with such stories," Masego said. "We live here."

While Afia understood his concern, she believed that Milele was worth telling Mufasa about. "Masego, that's what hope is. Light through the darkness."

When Mufasa reached the plains, he joined the other animals around the new craterlike watering hole, with liquid still raining from above and pooling at his feet from a nearby stream. He moved toward the center of the hole until most of his body had been covered with water. He lifted his head, watching the other animals enjoy the celebratory moment.

Giraffes gracefully leaned down, their elongated necks reaching toward the water's surface, while zebras, adorned in striking black-and-white patterns, trotted through the pooling reservoir. Mischievous monkeys filled the air with their playful antics, and many dove into the water. Their splashes created ripples that danced across the mirrored surface.

But Mufasa lost track of how quickly the water level was rising until he bobbed in a small wave, nearly losing his balance. He felt something nudge his back, and he saw a giraffe pushing him onto a large rock with its head. With the giraffe's help, Mufasa managed to climb atop the rock, and he said, "Thank you!"

The rain continued to intensify, drenching Mufasa's golden coat. Quickly the water rose to Mufasa's ankles, covering nearly all the rock and making it a danger rather than a refuge.

Afia, growing concerned, called out from the hilltop, "Mufasa, that's enough."

Mufasa's heart pounded as he gazed up at his parents, perched on the edge of the hill above.

Then a loud crack resounded from around the corner of the canyon, and it wasn't just thunder. The rumbling sound bolted toward the watering hole, and all the animals scrambled. Zebras leapt out of the water. Monkeys scurried onto higher ground. Birds took flight into the dark sky. Mufasa could only stay put, clinging to the disappearing rock, helplessly stuck.

"Mufasa, come back now!" Masego called out this time.

But it was too late. Mufasa looked directly up the ravine to find a massive wave, growing taller and taller as it barreled toward him. The wave crashed down on him and swept him under its powerful current.

Everything seemed to disappear. There was no sound. No sight.

And then Mufasa broke the surface of the water.

"Mufasa!" shouted Masego.

"Father!" Mufasa screamed at the top of his lungs.

Masego called out again, his voice cracking. "Mufasa!"

Mufasa tumbled and turned over in the rising water, struggling to find his bearings. The current dragged him farther and farther from the shore, and his energy dwindled.

Masego dashed down from the hilltop, quickly followed by Afia. Together they pushed through the stampede, dodging the hooves and horns of the animals as they ran. Mufasa's cries for help grew fainter in the distance. Afia's heart was in her throat as she saw him disappear beneath the surface of the water again.

Mufasa was swept back under the unforgiving and unpredictable water. Frantically flailing, he forced himself to the surface and called out again for his father. He caught a glimpse of his parents bobbing in the waves, trying their hardest to get to him. His heart thudded like the heavy footsteps of an elephant bull.

He managed to stay above the water by kicking his paws whichever way he could. Somehow he ended up washing onto a ledge on the far side of the watering hole, opposite from where he had run in. He could barely stand and nearly collapsed under the weight of his own drenched body.

Panting, Mufasa spoke to himself. "Come on, Mufasa, you can do this!"

Mufasa spotted his mother across the way, standing on a ledge on the opposite side of the water from him.

"Whoa!" said Mufasa. "That was close."

Then he saw his father in the water, still struggling. Masego swirled, his head whipping about as he willed himself against the current, holding on to hope. He was going to make it, but he had to keep his strength. Afia called out to him and went to help. She reached out a paw, while Mufasa could only stand on the opposite ledge and call out, "Dad!"

Mercifully, the current washed Masego onto the ledge beside Afia. But his concern was still his son. "Mufasa!"

Just as relief washed over Mufasa, happy to see his parents safe, the earth beneath him started eroding. He noticed two elephants trapped in the ravine barreling toward him. They, too, swirled in the water. Their massive bodies created big waves, waves big enough to cover half of the ledge where he stood. Mufasa had no choice but to move in the opposite direction of where his parents stood. But before he could get far, an elephant smashed into the side of an earthen dam nearby.

Boom!

The resulting rumble that pulsed through the ground sent even more water down the ravine, and this new flood swept up everything in its path. The ripple and rush of currents intersected, creating a burst of light and bubbles and froth and debris. It might be safer under the water than above it, where he'd be chancing another creature or the unruly floodwaters smashing him into the dam walls.

Whoosh!

Mufasa flung himself into the water.

CHAPTER 3: BEFORE

Mufasa tumbled like a leaf caught in the rapids of a raging river, falling beneath the water's surface. The water was cloudy, full of murky earth, and for a moment, Mufasa just drifted through it.

But slowly the water calmed and cleared, and eventually a branch miraculously floated up from the depths. Mufasa quickly grasped on to it, and it carried him upward until he finally broke the surface.

After Mufasa emerged above water into a starry night, he looked around in confusion. Though the rain had cleared up, and the air was only slightly windy, the water had flushed him far away, beyond where he'd come from. Where were the other animals? Where were his parents?

He desperately scanned the vast expanse of water for any sign of rescue or hope. As he clung to the branch to stay afloat, panic rose within him. Would he ever see his parents again?

Whoosh! A giant hippo surfaced beside him, snorting loudly. Mufasa held on to the branch like a lifeline, his claws digging deep into the bark. But the hippo just eyed him kindly.

A faint line of light appeared on the horizon, and eventually day broke. Mufasa continued to drift with the current as strange, unfamiliar sounds roared in his ears. He looked back toward the light, the world he had left behind, and felt fear course through him.

"Hello!" someone called.

Whirling around, Mufasa saw him: a small lion cub, perched on the high bank of the river in a regal posture that belied his youth. Mufasa swam closer, his heart pounding with a mixture of fear and excitement: a creature his own age! The cub watched him with a steady gaze, his tiny ears angled forward as if listening to some distant sound.

"I'm Taka—son of Obasi," the cub yelled from the shore, his tail twitching. "What's your name?"

"Mufasa!" he shouted back.

The river drifted leisurely now, and Mufasa bobbed gently in front of Taka.

"I'm not allowed to talk to outsiders—but I have a secret I really want to tell you," Taka said.

"What's the secret?" Mufasa asked.

"I'll get in trouble," Taka said playfully, almost taunting.

Tired of floating aimlessly, Mufasa begged, "Please, just tell me."

"Ah. I don't know," Taka said, glancing around to confuse Mufasa even more.

"Just tell me," Mufasa insisted.

Taka sighed and with a snort said, "Okay. You're about to be eaten!"

Mufasa glanced to his left and then his right and

shuddered: two crocodiles approached, submerged halfway in the water. Their snouts lifted above the surface, revealing their sharp yellowed teeth, and their big eyes hungrily protruded as they crept up on him. A single bite from those jaws could easily end his life.

"I hate secrets!" he yelled.

He took a big gulp of air and flailed toward the shore. But he was uncoordinated and fell off his branch, paws flapping about in the middle of the river.

"Swim!" Taka called out from the water's edge.

"But I can't!" Mufasa shouted, trying to stay afloat.

"You have to swim!" Taka repeated.

"I don't know how!"

As the crocodiles neared, Mufasa froze, panic and alarm rising through his body. He couldn't find his breath, and blood rushed to his face.

"All right, chin up," Taka said encouragingly. "Then walk underwater really fast!"

"I can't!" Mufasa yelled once more.

With the confidence of someone who faced no immediate danger, Taka replied, "Come on, Mufasa! Faster!"

Mufasa panicked again at the thought of his parents. They wouldn't have hesitated to jump in after him and scare the crocodiles away. He almost called out to them, but he stopped himself when he realized they were far, far away. He had never wanted more for them to come out from the brush and save him.

Mufasa's heart squeezed with terror as the two crocodiles surged toward him. He flailed his paws frantically, trying to swim away from the looming jaws that seemed to be closing in on him from all sides.

He tore his eyes away from the approaching doom and gazed at the shore. Although only a few feet away, it might as well have been miles. As he swam toward it, some water splashed into his mouth, making him cough and sputter. His lungs burned with exertion, and his strength ebbed away with every passing second.

Finally, Mufasa made it to the edge of the river and began to climb up toward dry land. He struggled as he got higher, and now he could see Taka up close; he was almost at the top.

"Help me, Taka!" he called. "Help me!"

For a moment, Mufasa thought that Taka might ignore him and let him be eaten by the crocodiles for his own entertainment. But then Taka reached out and grabbed the back of Mufasa's head with a small paw and pulled him to safety.

Another lion, this one an adult, charged in. She pounced and roared at the two crocodiles, sending them scurrying back into the river. Mufasa's weak legs barely held him up as he panted. The lioness rounded toward both him and Taka, her eyes showing a mixture of fury and worry that reminded Mufasa of his own mother.

"I told you to wait for me," she told Taka sternly.

"It's not my fault, Mom. I came down for a drink and saw him floating by." Taka pointed at the drenched Mufasa and shrugged. "I'd like you to meet Mufasa."

Taka's mother sighed, some tension leaving her body. "Oh, you're lucky those crocs were young and afraid to fight. Let's go!"

Taka didn't budge, staying staunchly at Mufasa's side.

Shaking off some of the water from his soaking wet fur, Mufasa stretched his limbs in various ways, trying to get out all the kinks that had built up in his body while he'd been flung around in the water.

"We can't just leave him here," said Taka.

"Rules are rules, Taka." The female lion looked toward Mufasa unforgivingly. "Obasi will never accept a stray."

Hearing the word *stray* raised Mufasa's hackles. "I'm not a stray. I'm just lost."

"See?" Taka agreed. "He's just lost!"

Mufasa's big eyes watered. "There was a flood. My parents—they tried to save me. Do you know which way is home?"

Taka's mother moved in closer to Mufasa. She searched his face and stared down at the tiny wet pile of courage.

"Home?" she repeated. "To be lost is to learn the way. Call me Eshe."

"I'm tired, Eshe," Mufasa told her.

"Come on!" said Taka. "It's this way!"

As Eshe and Taka started to walk off, Mufasa looked back toward the river—toward the faint light of a distant horizon. He sniffed the air, smelling nothing familiar. His heart clenched at the thought of home.

Taka looked back at him. "Come on, Mufasa!"

Mufasa joined them, and Taka bounced up to Eshe and asked her, "Mom, what's a stray?"

"Oh, Taka," Eshe said gently.

As Mufasa traipsed along with Eshe and Taka, he could not contain his curiosity. His eyes scanned the landscape around him: verdant wetlands and grass-covered hills stretching for miles. Trees abundantly dotted the expansive plains with plenty of glistening leaves. The birds sang peacefully as the sun shone through the dense foliage that covered them.

A question slipped from Mufasa's mouth subconsciously. "Is this . . . Milele?"

Eshe threw a curious look behind her. "No, my love."

As they made their way up toward the den, the grass grew taller and the trees became scarce. Taka and Eshe had been headed to the river for a catch, but they'd found

Mufasa instead. The lions guarding the entrance to the den watched as the trio approached. They looked imposing, their muscles rippling under their fur as they eyed the newcomer. Eshe and Taka exchanged wary glances but continued to approach, confident in their familiarity with the pride.

The guards moved aside to make way for a large male lion—Obasi, Mufasa guessed.

He seemed like a strong king but past his prime, with his mane tousled and his eyes a little red-rimmed, like he'd just woken up from a deep slumber.

He walked toward Eshe with steady steps. "I was trying to nap, Eshe, the all-important nap of kings! Only to be awoken by the disgusting, hideous, revolting stench of a stray! When we come upon an outsider—tell me, what do we do?"

Eshe did not back down. "Obasi—I know—"

His roar echoed throughout the land as he said, "*Eat it!*"

"But I found him, Dad," Taka chimed in, only a little bit scared. "I saved his life."

Obasi turned his nose up at his words. "Taka, we do not associate with outsiders! The only true bond is blood! I've heard stories of lions twice our size! These outsiders will devour everything in their path."

"Does he look like he's going to devour you?" Eshe asked, gesturing to Mufasa.

Obasi leaned down toward Mufasa, who shivered and cowered under his massive frame. Obasi sniffed Mufasa and reared his head back. "Well, that smell is disgusting! I'm not even sure I can eat this *kibeti*!"

Mufasa frowned. "I'm not a kibeti. I'm a Mufasa."

Obasi turned to Mufasa as his anger built up. "Do you even know what Mufasa means?"

Confused, Mufasa said, "No."

Obasi snorted. "It means 'king.' And that's me! You better start running, little Mufasa—for your life!"

"If I run, you'll never catch me," Mufasa snapped back. "I'm the fastest cub that ever lived. My father told me so."

Obasi cast a disdainful look at the small cub. "And how big was your father's pride?"

Mufasa's body puffed up. "It was me. And my mom."

Obasi lapped up Mufasa's words, laughing hysterically with his pride of lions.

"The son of a worthless nomad," the old king said. "Hey, perhaps you'd like to race my son? Because he has my blood—which makes him the fastest cub in the world. Taka—you have a challenge!"

The pride roared at the word *challenge*.

Taka felt a knot form in his stomach. He had never challenged another young cub before. He'd only wanted Mufasa to join the pride, and now he had no idea what was happening.

Mufasa had also never faced a challenge, and he only wanted a home. But if this was what he had to do to be accepted, Mufasa knew he could run.

"They will race to the Dead Tree and back!" said Obasi. He pointed out a tall, withering tree in the distance. "And when the prince defeats him, I will finish him in one bite!"

"What if Mufasa wins?" Eshe interrupted. "If he wins, he lives, Obasi. He stays with me."

Obasi contemplated the question for a second, staring Mufasa down while doing so. Then he finally came to a decision and announced in front of everyone, "You have my word."

CHAPTER 4: BEFORE

Taka and Mufasa stood shoulder to shoulder, their eyes fixed on the open expanse in front of them, ready to start the race. The lion pride looked on anxiously, unsure of which cub could outpace the other. The tension in the air was as palpable as the midday heat on the savannah.

Obasi stepped up to kick off the challenge. He sent out a mighty roar, marking the start of the race.

Mufasa and Taka both dug their paws into the dirt and lunged forward. Before Mufasa could get too far, Obasi swiped at Mufasa's hind legs and flipped him over, causing Mufasa to trip and fall flat onto his back. The entire pride of lions erupted into laughter as Mufasa grunted from breathing in the dust.

"Clumsy little stray," Obasi taunted.

Eshe was unable to find any humor in the situation. Her eyes filled with sorrow. She moved forward to help the fallen cub and shouted, "Run, Mufasa!"

Taka's rapid pace began to falter as he noticed Mufasa struggling to regain his footing. He yearned to win the race, but he also felt genuine concern for his fallen competitor. Despite his hesitation, Taka pressed on, his heart heavy with regret. He knew that his victory was likely.

Even though Mufasa was humiliated, he wanted to prove all the others wrong. He knew he was fast, just like his father had told him. He summoned energy from the depths of his soul, imagining his parents' voices as he pushed past the pain and exhaustion throughout his body.

Mufasa drove his paws into the dirt, slowly closing the distance between himself and Taka with wide jumps. The other lions watched with bated breath.

As Eshe watched Mufasa catch up to Taka, she told Obasi, "You did not have to do that."

Obasi scoffed. "Taka is the future—he has to win his first challenge."

Eshe shook her head. "No, Obasi, to be a true king, he must earn it. Don't take that away from him."

The two cubs shrank into dots on the savannah plain as they got farther and farther away.

Taka held his advantage, and he knew the terrain. After all, this was his home, and he had spent many days playing here as an only child. He knew every rock, every crevice, and every hidden path. He knew how to navigate through the wetlands along the creek and the blotches of acacia trees that crisscrossed the way.

As Mufasa bounded toward Taka, he could feel the wind rushing past him, carrying the scents of the savannah and the distant roar of a waterfall. His powerful muscles flexed beneath his fur, propelling him forward with effortless grace.

Despite the blazing sun beating down, Mufasa felt exhilarated. Every heartbeat echoed in his chest like a drum, urging him onward, and his breath came in quick, ragged gasps. But even as his muscles burned with the effort, he remained focused and determined. Mufasa never gave up.

Taka moved down to the edge of a shallow canal. Mufasa followed until his ankles met the water. A chill spread over his entire body, and he froze. Flashes filled his mind: of the elephant crashing into the earthen levee, releasing the torrent of water that had separated him from his mother and father.

He couldn't give up; he had to find a way around the water. His eyes traveled upward to the trees lining the canal and landed on a long branch just above him, which led to another and another. He wasted no time jumping onto it and started to run across. The thick branches bent with Mufasa's weight but held strong. Now he was running parallel to Taka instead of behind him.

Mufasa's heart pounded as he raced to the end of the line of branches. The wind carried the scent of leaves and soil, and his eyes flickered as he saw the flooded ditch looming below him. For a moment, doubt crept into his mind: could he make the jump and avoid the water? Perhaps not, but he didn't have time to mull it over. He forced the fear aside and focused on the task at hand.

With a fierce growl, Mufasa launched himself off the edge, adrenaline rushing through him as he soared through the air. Time seemed to slow down as he sailed over the ditch, his eyes locked on the ground below.

And then, with a thud that jolted his entire body, he landed in the ditch. With a burst of energy, he scrambled out of the ditch just as Taka sped by and said, "Better hurry!"

So Mufasa did, pouncing away from the ditch to run side by side with Taka through the tall grass. The two cubs sprinted onward, pushing themselves to run faster than they ever had before.

Just when they approached the finish line, Taka looked at Mufasa and said, "I have one more secret, Mufasa."

Then Taka began to slow down, and Mufasa tilted his head, confused by Taka's sluggish and uncoordinated gait. Mufasa watched over his shoulder as the distance between them grew wider.

"I always wanted a brother," Taka shouted behind him.

Taka's unexpected words echoed in Mufasa's mind as he approached the waiting pride. Yards ahead, he saw Obasi step into his path. Mufasa shifted his direction and fixed his eyes on Eshe.

He did not stop until he reached her.

Mufasa panted ferociously as he caught his breath. His fur was matted with dirt, but he had won the race.

Taka caught up and pounced on Mufasa playfully, congratulating him. Joy eased across Mufasa's face. He had never thought about having a brother, but now it seemed like it might be fun!

The furious Obasi stalked up to the two cubs playing and swiped Mufasa away from Taka before shouting, "Cheater!"

Eshe immediately jumped in to defend Mufasa. "Obasi!"

The pride watched their king with keen eyes, anticipating his next move. Obasi had given his permission to
let Mufasa stay if he won, and if he went back on his word
now, the entire pride surely would lose the respect they
held for him.

Obasi looked back at his pride and begrudgingly
accepted what he must do.

"You will keep him with the females," Obasi said, and
then he tensed up again and turned toward Taka. "Taka,
how could you lose to a stray?"

Taka bowed his head in shame. Obasi turned his back
to his son and walked away. As the king went farther and
farther away, Taka's eyes slowly lifted, and he smiled con-
spiratorially, his shame clearly pretend. He bumped into
Mufasa and resumed playing with him.

"I thought you said you were fast," he said, taunting
Mufasa. "I had to let you win!"

"Well, I did just go days with no sleep while riding the
waves of a flood halfway across the continent," Mufasa
snorted.

Taka danced around him, seemingly in pure bliss

even after the loss and his father's challenge. "Excuses, excuses, excuses."

Taka's only wish had come true. He had felt alone on the savannah, with no siblings or close friends to share his adventures with. But now, as he ran and played with Mufasa, he had a sense of kinship and belonging that he had never experienced before.

Eshe watched from a distance, impressed by the new bond that was forming between the two young cubs. She had never seen Taka happier.

"Anyway, come on, Mufasa," said Taka. "Let's get into some trouble!"

CHAPTER 5: BEFORE

From then on, Taka and Mufasa continued their mischievous escapades, relishing their youthful exuberance. They explored the savannah each day with newfound energy, as if they were seeing the world for the first time. They scampered through the tall grasses, chasing each other, and leapt over small shrubs and bushes. And though Mufasa missed his old home and his parents, as time went by, he felt more and more at ease in this new place.

Taka and Mufasa's adventures were as boundless as the vast plains they called home. However, time marched on, and with each passing day, the cubs grew older, wiser, and more curious about the world that lay beyond their familiar playground.

Days danced into months, and months melted into years. Soon the once-playful cubs were young adults, their bodies lengthened and their manes starting to hint at their regal potential.

Although the cubs stood a bit taller now, their gazes sparkled with the same mischief and adventure. The passage of time had not dulled their spirits but instead fueled a newfound desire for exploration and pushing the boundaries of their world.

One day, Taka and Mufasa hid amid the tall grass, eyeing the sleeping male lions ahead of them under the Shade Tree. The younger lions crept toward the pride, blending in with the dead silence.

Then, suddenly, Mufasa pounced toward them, announcing, "Elephant stampede!"

Taka pounced in next to Mufasa, adding, "Run for your lives!"

The lions jolted from their daytime nap; some clawed up the tree's trunk and others jumped into the branches.

Fear flashed in their eyes until they realized it had only been a prank.

"Chigaru jumped like twenty feet," Mufasa said with a laugh, gesturing to a lion who now hid in the tree branches.

"That's a new record!" Taka added.

"Obasi," complained Chigaru, still hiding in the tree, "they did it again! Your sons are nothing but trouble."

Obasi cowered behind the Shade Tree, ashamed. He pointed to Mufasa. "That one is not my son!"

Chigaru shook his head. "They're heathens, the both of them!"

Obasi growled low. "This stray is forbidden to be near the Shade Tree."

"Mufasa and I were just playing . . ." Taka began, standing up for his brother.

Obasi reared his head and roared. "Do not say his name, Taka! I won't let his cowardly blood corrupt you! You two will never be brothers!" He turned toward Mufasa. "Now go back to the females. And stay away from my son."

Obediently, the two brothers split up—Mufasa heading for the high grass, toward the female lions, and Taka remaining at the Shade Tree.

"Oh, your mother, she adopts every lizard, speaks to passing grasshoppers," Obasi told Taka.

Taka did not much like the company of his bitter father. Obasi always bad-mouthed someone, even his son's mother.

"I want to go with him!" Taka protested.

Obasi's red-rimmed eyes flashed with anger. "You want to be with the females. You belong with the males."

"He gets to hunt with Mother . . ." Taka said, thinking about all the time Mufasa had spent stalking prey next to Eshe over the years.

"One day he will betray you. That is what strays do."

But Taka remained adamant. "Mufasa would—"

"Hey, hey." Obasi lowered himself to Taka and nuzzled him. "This will all be yours, my son." Obasi lifted his head and gestured to the expansive savannah plains. "You will be king. So pay attention, and study every move I make!"

Then Obasi dramatically lay down in the shade, passed gas, and closed his eyes.

"Sleeping?" cried Taka. "Again!"

"That is what males do," Obasi said. "We protect the pride as we nap! That's, well, that's power!"

Obasi's words echoed through Taka's soul. Taka whispered, "Power," trying to find meaning in what his father had just told him.

The pride of lions stretched out under the Shade Tree. Taka stared at them lounging lazily under the canopy of leaves and then looked off in the opposite direction, where he could see Mufasa and Eshe going toward the meadows. He wished with all his heart that he could join them.

As they disappeared from view, the sound of their footsteps faded away, leaving only the soft rustling of the grasses and the distant calls of birds to fill the air.

After crossing the clearing that looked out over the Valley of Kings, Eshe settled down.

Curious, Mufasa asked, "Why are we stopping?"

Eshe replied, "Close your eyes—and tell me what you hear. What you feel."

Mufasa closed his eyes and sniffed the air. After a beat, he replied, "There's a herd of antelope heading across the dry lake bed—about half a day from here."

Eshe looked at him with pride. "And how do you know they're not gazelles?"

Concentrating once again, Mufasa said, "Their steps are too heavy—moving way too slow."

Eshe made a low noise in her throat in agreement. "What else? Come on; you can do it."

Mufasa replied, "When the wind hits their horns, it moves up instead of across. So definitely antelope horns."

Eshe nodded. "Very good."

Mufasa turned away from her and sniffed the air again.

Eshe asked, "What is it, Mufasa? What's wrong?"

Mufasa shook his head, not wanting to say but deciding to share anyway. "Sometimes I get a scent—it's barely a trace on the wind. And it smells like . . . home."

For a moment, his parents' faces flashed through his mind.

"And then it's gone," he said sadly.

Eshe smiled gently. "Mufasa, your parents—we can keep looking farther downriver. . . ."

Mufasa lowered his gaze, not wanting Eshe to see the sadness in his eyes. "They're gone, Eshe. You're wasting your time training me like this!"

She looked him squarely in the eyes. "But these skills you have—no other male has them."

Mufasa pawed the grassy meadow, petulant. "Obasi will never accept me; I'll never be his blood. His family."

Eshe's eyes grew soft. "But you are my family. And if Obasi could see how gifted you are . . ."

"Well, maybe I like being a stray. No rules—no responsibility. I'm the lucky one, Eshe."

"What do you mean, Mufasa?" Eshe snapped.

"I never have to be like Taka," he said. He turned to walk away but said one last thing before he left the meadow: "I never have to be king."

CHAPTER 6: NOW (INTERLUDE)

"**D**id he say no rules? And no responsibility?" asked Pumbaa, interrupting the story. The question hung in the air, momentarily disrupting the flow of Rafiki's narration.

Caught up in their own chatter, Timon and Pumbaa bubbled with excitement, and soon they couldn't contain themselves any longer. In true meerkat and warthog fashion, they burst into a spirited song, their voices filling the air as they celebrated the notion of a life without rules or responsibilities.

Amid the animated conversation and melodious cacophony, Kiara couldn't help feeling a mixture of annoyance and curiosity. She knew she had to regain control of the situation and find out what happened next in the story. She inhaled deeply, then let out a resounding yell: "*Quiet!*"

Timon and Pumbaa, taken aback by the sudden outburst, promptly quieted, their chatter reduced to grumbling whispers.

"Rafiki," Kiara instructed with a firm yet respectful tone, "keep going."

Rafiki, nodding appreciatively at Kiara's intervention, resumed his narration. With a gleam in his eyes and a mischievous smile playing on his lips, he continued weaving the tale, capturing everyone's attention once again. "Later that day, Eshe was teaching Mufasa how to hunt in pairs. But on this day, something was hunting them. . . ."

As Rafiki's words danced into their ears, they leaned forward, eager to follow the unfolding narrative, and their imaginations began running wild with curiosity and excitement.

CHAPTER 7: BEFORE

Eshe knew Mufasa needed a distraction, so she took him farther into the savannah to finesse his hunting skills. Eshe padded on light paws, jumping and avoiding fallen tree branches while lurking low to the ground, and Mufasa followed her, stepping where she stepped. He watched in awe as Eshe gracefully stalked prey and moved through the debris, her muscles rippling beneath her tawny coat. What Eshe could do without even looking required much more attention and effort from Mufasa.

Eshe ran up the steep cliff without any difficulty and stopped at the edge of the clearing. She eyed a herd of impalas munching the grass, then looked back at Mufasa, waiting on his haunches, and motioned with a bob of her head for him to crouch low.

Mufasa wasted no time in bolting to the other side of the clearing, his paws landing on the grassy terrain without making a single sound.

Eshe crouched down opposite him between two trees and saw the crown of Mufasa's head moving through the grass directly across from her, nearly camouflaged. Then, breathing lightly through her nose, she leveled her eyes at the herd of impalas. Her muscles tightened as she prepared herself for the plunge, awaiting the right moment to make the move.

Her ears stood straight up, ready for the attack.

But unbeknownst to either of them, they had been followed.

Concealed, Taka crouched even lower behind Mufasa, mirroring his brother's every move in the thick grass. Taka giggled to himself, knowing how skilled he must have been to fool even his mother. But he would do whatever it took to learn her hunting secrets.

What he didn't realize was that while he was watching his mother and Mufasa, the male lion Chigaru stalked even farther behind him, watching him.

Eshe dug her paws into the ground, about to pounce toward an impala that walked some distance ahead of its herd.

Then another noise sounded nearby—not from the herd of impalas—and she froze. She slowly turned around and found herself confronted by two massive white lions emerging from the high grasses. Her eyes widened, and her mouth opened as a low growl built up at the base of her throat.

She raked her eyes over the lions' massive frames and noticed that she had never encountered the likes of them before. Their pure white coats were streaked with dark red blood from a recent kill. Eshe's heart thudded as she took a couple of steps back, her legs almost giving out. She did not want to glance toward Mufasa. That would tell them that she wasn't alone, and maybe they'd go after him.

The two lions approached Eshe with slow, deliberate

steps, their muscles rippling under their white coats. Their mouths hung open, revealing a dazzling array of razor-sharp teeth that glinted menacingly in the sunlight. Eshe knew she had to act fast, but her legs felt heavy and uncooperative. She struggled to keep her breathing steady, even as her mind raced with thoughts of escape.

With a burst of adrenaline, Eshe sprinted toward the nearby field, her legs pumping furiously. She could hear the lions close behind her, their hot breath washing over her as they closed in for the kill. Eshe willed herself to run faster, to outrun the hunters and escape to safety . . . and with a fierce roar, Eshe reached the clearing's center.

"Run!" she shouted.

The impalas scattered, starting a stampede that lifted dust and panic into the air, but it was too late for Eshe. The white lions caught her tail and pinned her down.

Taka stood frozen in the grass as lions twice his mother's size attacked her. He took a few steps ahead, wanting to help his mother. Then he retreated with his ears flattened and tail tucked between his legs. A whine built up at the back of Taka's throat as fear coursed through him.

Eshe extended her nails and swiped at one of the white lions. As the second one leapt toward her, she swiped him, too, bringing both of them to the ground. Eshe stood with her teeth bared, pressing her paws firmly into the earth.

Then Mufasa leapt from the grasses and in between Eshe and the white lions. Eshe bled where one of the lions had managed to bite her, but she tried to tell Mufasa to back down and run away for help. He didn't listen, and the white lions lunged onto him.

At the other end of the clearing, Taka, driven by terror, ran back toward the Shade Tree as distant roars filled the valley. He tightened his jaw, dispelling the urge to give a howl of his own.

Mufasa rolled through the dirt, and his vision blurred with dust. The white lions' quick attacks gave him no time to escape. He panted as his eyes moved back and forth, from one lion to the other, gauging their next move. The white lions took just a moment longer before flogging Mufasa again, giving him the chance to inch away and stand on his feet.

The white lions planted themselves in front of Mufasa, ready to send him back to the ground. Mufasa, while the smallest in this battle, stood with his forelegs bent for momentum and hind legs stretched out. His form appeared to be just as good as his enemies'. He bared his teeth and narrowed his eyes as he growled, a warning to stay put. But the white lions didn't listen.

Eshe swallowed a whimper and hid her pain, standing side by side with Mufasa. The white lions' attacks kept coming without pause. But Mufasa noticed one of the branches of a nearby tree hung low, and it appeared to have been sharpened by the disturbance of every passing animal. Mufasa backed one of the white lions against the branch, then tripped him, making him fall into the pointed stick. The white lion burst into howls until only silence hung in the space.

As Mufasa returned to Eshe's side to fend off the

other lion, another figure made its way through the dust gathered around them. Mufasa's eyes widened when he saw Chigaru. Chigaru's lips curled back, and thick saliva dripped from his sharp canines as he dared the remaining white lion to make another move.

The white lion stopped in his tracks and then took a few steps back. He spared Mufasa one last glance, eyes closed in slits, and then he dashed away. Before Mufasa and Eshe could breathe a sigh of relief and thank Chigaru, he took off to pursue the escaped white lion. Mufasa watched the stoic lion go and wondered if he should follow.

"Mufasa!" Eshe said. "Always be mindful of your rage. When your thoughts are clear, you cease to become prey."

Chigaru soon returned from his chase, having driven off the other lion. Mufasa nudged Eshe, who was no longer attempting to hide her injuries, and he helped her regain her balance while ignoring his own injuries. She struggled to walk and gritted her teeth with each step. In silence, the three lions headed toward the Shade Tree.

Under the Shade Tree's expansive foliage, Obasi paced back and forth, his chest puffed out. Behind him stood Taka, and behind both of them lined up the entire pride, waiting for the return of Eshe, Mufasa, and Chigaru.

When Obasi spotted the three lions on the ridge above the tree, his eyes went immediately to their wounds. The trio rejoined the pride, and Mufasa collapsed beneath the tree.

Eshe turned toward Obasi and spoke in a low voice, "Obasi, they were huge—white as ghosts—like nothing I've seen before."

While Mufasa remained quiet, Chigaru did not miss the opportunity to say, his voice carrying over to the masses, "Mufasa took on two by himself!"

Eshe looked toward Mufasa, her eyes shining. "Yes, he did."

"One of them is dead!" Chigaru continued to boast.

As the crowd murmured about the incident and Mufasa's bravery, a dejected Taka watched as Obasi walked past him—and, to the surprise of everyone present, straight for Mufasa. The pride watched silently as Obasi moved closer to the stray.

Obasi tightened his jaw as his paws clenched the soft ground. "I owe you a great debt . . . Mufasa."

Everyone gasped as Obasi used Mufasa's name for the first time.

Mufasa slowly got to his feet, clearly in pain, and rose to Obasi's level. "We need to prepare," he said, his voice hardened to match the gravity of the news. "They're downwind—less than a day away."

This brought on more discussion in the pride as Obasi sniffed the wind before whirling around. "No, you couldn't possibly know this."

Mufasa shrugged. "Send a scout and you'll see. They'll be coming for us."

Obasi turned to look at Chigaru sternly, a clear indication to go and scout the area. Chigaru ran off in an instant.

Taka approached Obasi. "Father . . . I'm sorry."

"Not here," replied Obasi. "Not now."

Obasi stomped off, and Taka watched him go, crushed and disappointed in himself.

"It's okay, Taka," said Eshe. "Come, my son."

∧∨∧∨∧

Some miles away from Obasi's pride, the injured white lion limped past dead animals and rows of fresh carcasses scattered on the savannah floor. They weren't the bones of zebras and gazelles, but instead of an entire pride of lions. Vultures covered the land, picking off what remains they found.

The injured white lion approached his blue-eyed king, Kiros, who stood on a ridge eyeing the sunset, his back to the blood-coated lion.

The king spoke in a scratchy voice. "Where is my son?"

The injured white lion sniveled and bent down before the king. "There was a young lion, Majesty—he fought Shaju."

Kiros roared, making the lion flinch. "You see the bones at my feet? They are the kings who once ruled this valley. I've tasted them all. And you're telling me one little lion killed my son?"

The white lion whimpered. "We fought as best we could—but there were others!"

Pacing across the ridge in slow steps, he spoke in a low, measured voice. "And yet you came back. You survived?"

The lion stooped so low his nose rubbed the ground. "I was badly hurt! I promise, Majesty—this is the truth!"

"The truth . . ." Kiros scoffed.

"Yes, the truth," the injured white lion meekly replied.

Kiros gave a sinister smile. "The truth is standing behind you."

Two large females stepped forward and circled the injured lion. Known as "the hunters," these two could smell a lie. They looked straight out of someone's nightmares, their faces stained with the blood of a kill.

The injured lion, belly pressed flat to the ground, choked out, "No . . . no . . . no . . ."

They studied the injured lion as they sniffed at his fur.

One of them, Amara, cackled sharply. "There were others, Majesty."

The other, Akua, grunted. "But only one left blood on his mane."

They both came together to stand in front of the injured lion as Amara concluded with her head held high, "Which means *he* left Shaju to die."

"Saved himself," Akua added.

"This young lion—was he their king?" Kiros asked, walking down the ridge slowly.

"His blood is common, ordinary," Amara said.

Kiros growled loudly. "Answer me! Was he their king?"

Akua bowed her head in respect before answering, "No, Majesty, you are the only king."

Menacingly, the pride began to surround the injured lion, staring at him with their sharp teeth exposed. As the circle of white lions constricted on its prey like a snake, vultures took to the sky.

CHAPTER 8: BEFORE

As the rest of the pride dispersed and Chigaru scouted for the white lions, Taka, still embarrassed by his own weakness, left the flat ground behind and traversed into the sinking sun to be alone. He trudged through the tall grasses of the savannah to a nearby hill, his head hung low in shame.

He had always prided himself on his bravery and loyalty, but when it had mattered most, he had run away like a coward. Everyone now knew that Mufasa could protect Taka's family better than he could. Taka sniffled as he rubbed his paws on the ground again and again until a dent formed. He burrowed into it, trying to hide from the rest of the world.

Taka heard soft footsteps behind him and got up in a wink. Obasi was climbing up the steep hill. The Shade Tree stood tall behind him as he left its shadows and made his way to the top of the hill.

As the light dimmed, Obasi turned to stare at his son soberly. He nudged Taka to get him to look at him and then grunted out, "No one can ever know you ran. That you ran from your mother. It never happened, Taka—do you understand?"

Taka stared at his father. "But I didn't know. I was just scared."

"It doesn't matter," Obasi continued. "We must protect the bloodline. Protect the truth."

Finding the musky scent of the dirt and sand around him oddly comforting, he asked, "Protect them with a lie? That's deceitful."

"Deceit is the tool of a great king, Taka," said Obasi, trying to reason with the sad youth. "It's . . . what kings must do."

The word *king* echoed relentlessly in Taka's mind, as if mocking him. Despite Obasi's suggestion that his fate had been secured, Taka couldn't help feeling like he was the farthest away from the title. "But I am not a king. I'm just your son."

Silence hung in the space between them.

And then, from the base of the hill, they heard: "Obasi!"

"Chigaru?" Obasi shouted back.

"Obasi!" Chigaru called again.

His ears standing up in alarm, Obasi raced down the hill, with Taka following closely behind. Taka had never seen his father run so fast. They moved quickly and reached the gulch of the Shade Tree in no time, Obasi and Chigaru still shouting each other's names until Chigaru appeared on the ridge just above them.

Obasi leapt forward. "Chigaru, I'm here. What did you see?"

"They're coming this way, Obasi," Chigaru reported frantically. "Two lions for every one of ours! Each one bigger than the next! But none as mighty as their king . . ."

Obasi stepped forward, closer to his shuffling pride as they started to talk among themselves. After a solemn beat, he said, "Outsiders. The stories were all true."

Eshe made her way from the crowd and called in a booming voice that reverberated across the area: "We will fight with you, Obasi. Take the high ground—surprise them!"

"They'll arrive with the sunrise," Chigaru added.

Obasi paced the length of the Shade Tree's canopy, preoccupied with how he would protect his pride. The threat was growing nearer, and he had given no clear orders, which diminished his power as king. He fidgeted and nervously scanned the surroundings, searching for a solution. The weight of his responsibility pressed heavily on his shoulders, and he wondered if he was truly fit to lead his people in such dangerous times.

One thought remained at the forefront of his mind, and he spoke it aloud: "I must protect the bloodline, Eshe—the future of this pride."

Obasi approached his son. "Taka—you are that future. . . ."

Taka's brows knit together with growing apprehension. He shifted his weight, his body betraying the anxiety he felt inside. "Future? Dad—what do you mean?"

"I'm sending you away—far from here," said Obasi. "You will leave and start a new life. A new beginning."

Taka searched Obasi's face. "I don't understand. What are you asking me to do? What are you trying to tell me?"

"Run away, Taka! Run away—and never return," Obasi barked, and then walked over to Mufasa.

Seeing Taka's pain, Eshe filled the space left by Obasi and approached her son to comfort him, licking him as he shivered.

Obasi stood solemnly in front of Mufasa, regarding him finally as someone worthy to be in a king's presence. "I need you to go with him, Mufasa. To pledge your loyalty."

"I won't leave Eshe," Mufasa protested, his voice loud and firm. Mufasa regarded the lioness as his mother. She had taken him under her wing when everyone scoffed at him and called him a stray.

Though she was touched by Mufasa's words, Eshe said, "But, Mufasa, they will never stop looking for him."

Obasi stepped in closer and said, "They will track the bloodline. Mufasa, if you save Taka, you save this pride. You save Eshe. She lives in him."

Mufasa only gazed at both of them, knowing he would have to make an impossible choice.

∧∨∧∨∧

As the sun rose over the horizon, Mufasa joined Eshe at a ridge to the left of the Shade Tree. He still didn't want to leave her. Perhaps he could reason with her once more. She stared at the expanding land below as the pride moved about, preparing for the day ahead.

"I won't run, Eshe," said Mufasa. "We're staying to fight with you."

Eshe looked at him with half-opened eyes, still a bit tired. "This is not your fight. It's not. This is my fight. My time. And if you leave now, you'll still have a chance."

Mufasa whipped his head in her direction. "A chance?"

Eshe nodded, staring back out at the horizon. "To find your way home."

The word *home* clenched Mufasa's heart as the memories rushed back.

"Without you, I have no home. . . ." Mufasa nearly choked.

He knew that if he left, he'd never see Eshe again.

Eshe rubbed her chin on Mufasa's forehead. "You and Taka together—that is home."

Mufasa whispered, his voice breaking, "Eshe . . ."

Eshe refused to look at him, knowing that it would only cause her heartache. "Mufasa, look out there—beyond the light. There is a place my mother told me about, a place beyond the river's end—across the deepest canyon on the other side of the mountains. A place beyond the horizon itself. Yes, a pride lands so green, so perfect, that to see it is to see—"

"Milele."

Eshe nodded. "Yes. Yes. Forever . . ."

Mufasa remembered, all those years ago, his mother telling him about a place just like the one Eshe was describing. His eyes misted over as her echoing voice rang through his memories—and he thought of how he'd believed every word she'd said. Older now, he knew better.

"My mother told me this story," Mufasa said. "I'm not a cub, Eshe—"

"It's not a story," said Eshe. "Milele is home and it's in our blood—"

"I don't have your blood," Mufasa said.

"Oh, if only you knew," said Eshe. "You have more than that, Mufasa. You have my love. My son."

Eshe's heart ached for the danger that possibly lay ahead for Mufasa, Taka, and the rest of the pride, but she trusted Obasi's judgment. Mufasa and Taka had to leave.

She encouraged him with a nod as her own eyes filled with sadness. "Go. Go, Mufasa. Find your forever. . . ."

Taka appeared behind them and stepped toward his mother. "Mother, please forgive me. I beg of you . . ."

"There's no need, my love," Eshe said. "Taka, your moment of courage will come."

And though they had never wanted to leave their mother this way, both lions knew they needed to do as she said—and grant this final request.

Eshe's heart broke into a million tiny pieces because she knew she would never see either of them again.

"Now, both of you go. Go and find your place in the Circle of Life," she said, her voice cracking.

Mufasa and Taka began running toward their future, slowly looking back at Eshe. They were stepping into the unknown, forging their own paths, and embracing the challenges and triumphs that awaited them.

It was bittersweet for Eshe, knowing that she had played a significant role in shaping their lives but accepting that it was time to let them go.

Obasi came to stand beside her, though he remained as stoic as ever as he watched the two young lions fade into the grasses. As unemotional as he seemed, he understood the depth of Eshe's love for them. Together they stood as a united front, ready to face the challenges that lay ahead for the pride.

Obasi positioned himself in front of the pride, Eshe

right next to him. Suddenly he caught sight of movement in the distance: a group of white lions approaching. Obasi and Eshe exchanged looks of devotion. They knew what was coming, but they would stand their ground.

The rest of the pride saw Obasi's cautious stare out into the savannah and stood with him, forming a defensive line behind their king.

The white lions charged toward the Shade Tree. Kiros, the largest one and clearly the leader, moved toward Obasi, who was rooted to his spot, all of the fur on his body standing up. The two kings faced each other, and while he wished he were as menacing, Obasi couldn't help being terrified.

Kiros spoke first, nearly barking. "Which one of you is king?"

Obasi took a few steps closer to Kiros, standing nose to nose with him. "You have no reason to challenge me."

"Does this look like a challenge, King?" Kiros scoffed.

Obasi snarled at him. "There are rules among lions!"

Kiros cackled. "Not anymore. While you rule this pride, I've built my army. Yours is the last pride in the

Valley of Kings. Which means everything the light touches belongs to me! There will be one ruler. One lion king."

Kiros towered over Obasi, who cowered in his shadow.

"Now, which one of you kibeti killed my son?" the white lion demanded.

"We are not kibetis," replied Obasi.

Kiros glowered. "Oh, is that so?"

Obasi's heart seemed to be lodged in his throat as he choked out, "Forgive me, King."

The two hunters of King Kiros stepped forward, sniffing the air.

"He's not here," Amara said.

"There were two of them," added Akua. "They left together over that ridge."

"Lions don't hunt lions," Obasi said.

Kiros huffed as he came to stand in front of Obasi, baring his teeth at him. "Ohhhhhh, but they do now."

The white lions dropped their jaws at once and encircled Obasi and his pride—a ritual immediately familiar to the scout Chigaru, for he had witnessed the injured white lion meet the same fate the previous day. Obasi knew the pride would have to summon every ounce of strength and courage to stand a chance against this formidable adversary.

CHAPTER 9: BEFORE

Mufasa and Taka ran together, their hearts pounding as they fled across the meadow. The grasses whipped past them, and the wildflowers blurred together in a haze of colors. Several roars emerged from the direction of the Shade Tree. Mufasa and Taka stopped and looked over their shoulders, but they couldn't see anything.

"We have to move," Mufasa said, locking eyes with Taka. "They'll be tracking us."

Mufasa started to run again, but Taka stood unmoving. The thought of something happening to his parents frightened him deeper.

Mufasa leapt over to him and bumped his head into Taka's shoulder. "Taka!"

Taka snapped out of his thoughts. "No, maybe they ran away. We should go back to the pride—"

Mufasa softened his gaze. "There is no going back. You're the pride now. You are Obasi. You are Eshe."

Mufasa felt exactly as Taka did, but now Mufasa had to step forward and carry out Eshe's wishes. They were no longer young cubs. They were on the verge of adulthood and had been trusted to carry the pride's legacy.

Taka's mouth wobbled. "What if you're wrong? What if they're okay . . ."

Mufasa studied Taka's face, then lifted a paw and said, "Taka! They live in you now! We may be surrounded by darkness, but brighter days will come, I promise you. Now follow me, brother. We have to move. Together."

A series of thunderous roars resounded from afar. Taka's muscles tensed, and his fur stood on end. The birds nearby took flight in a frenzy of loudly flapping wings. Mufasa and Taka exchanged quick glances before turning their backs to the source of the roars and taking off in a run.

Together the young lions wove through the thick undergrowth beneath the trees, with the sun streaking through the canopy above them and beating down mercilessly on their backs. The branches scraped and clawed at their fur, but fueled by a desperate need to escape the danger and carry their pride's hope, the duo didn't slow down.

Panting, Taka began to lag, doing his best to keep up with the faster Mufasa. Finally, Mufasa motioned for Taka to stop. His ears perked up as he sniffed at the air.

His eyes widened as he whispered, "Hunters . . ."

Taka shivered. "What's the plan?"

Mufasa looked behind him where the smell had come from and replied, "Uh . . . run very fast!"

Taka followed closely as they sprinted farther beneath the trees. The sound of twigs cracking and leaves rustling grew louder behind them until the hunters released an earth-shaking roar. Taka and Mufasa refused to look back again; they only pressed forward.

"This way!" Mufasa yelled.

Mufasa and Taka burst through the canopy of the trees and into a clearing next to a river. Instinctively, Taka hopped toward the rocky shore of the river, but Mufasa stopped at the sight of the water. He was paralyzed as he relived his last memory of his parents, standing on the other side of that flash flood.

Mufasa's heart pounded. He took a few steps away and pleaded, "Back to the trees . . ."

"We're trapped. We have to swim," Taka said fiercely, vetoing him.

Mufasa pulled back more from the water. "No. We have to fight."

"If we fight, we die," Taka said.

"But if we swim, we drown," Mufasa retorted.

Taka sighed, trying to find words to get Mufasa to agree. His eyes lit up as he said, "Okay. I didn't want to do this. But I command you to swim!"

"You what?"

Taka puffed out his chest. "You pledged your loyalty! I command you to swim!"

Mufasa's face hardened like a stone. "Taka—this is not the time for jokes."

A roar cut their conversation short. A group of white lions emerged from the trees, Kiros among them—and his eyes narrowed into slits as he gazed at Mufasa and Taka.

Kiros roared once more. "Which one of you killed my son?"

Mufasa had pledged to protect Taka's life. He stepped forward.

"I did," he said. "This lion with me is nothing but a stray. Let him go...."

"The other is no stray," Akua said.

The white lions started crossing the length of the meadow, getting closer by the second.

Amara sniffed the air once and added, "He holds the blood of the pride."

Kiros wiped the blood around his mouth with his tongue and said, "The last blood of a king. Hmmm..." He turned to the hunters and roared, "Blood for blood!"

The two hunters leapt toward Mufasa and Taka. The young lions dashed toward the river, the white lions on their heels. As the white lions cut them off, Mufasa swallowed his fear and leapt onto a boulder in the river. Then he leapt to another, carefully crossing the river like he was competing in a tactical agility race. Taka followed right behind him, using the same path.

They made their way across the river at the top of the falls. Mufasa shivered, the sight of water sending a new terror through him. But the thought of whom he needed to protect helped him move past his fear, and he continued forward, evading the white lions.

The white lions started leaping from boulder to boulder, too. Their strides were wide and powerful, and they made their jumps effortlessly.

When Mufasa and Taka reached the river's edge, with the hunters hot on their heels, they found themselves on a rocky plateau atop a waterfall, a four-hundred-foot sheet of falling water cutting off their path.

Taka's eyes flicked nervously over his shoulder. "They're coming!"

Mufasa scanned their surroundings for a way to escape. He gasped as an idea occurred to him. "We have the advantage!"

Taka squinted. "What advantage? We are on a rock in the middle of the water."

The white lions approached the edge of the island as Mufasa said, "Taka, this is it! We go for the king!"

Mist rose up from the massive waterfall behind them. Mufasa locked eyes with Kiros a few feet away.

Taka whispered, "Mufasa, I'm ready. Just one last thing."

"What?" Mufasa said slyly.

Taka whispered a quick "Chin up!"

He clamped Mufasa by the back of his neck and pulled them both over the edge.

Mufasa wheezed, "*Taka—*"

"This was a bad idea!" cried Taka.

As they hurtled down the waterfall, Taka and Mufasa clung to each other in a tangled mess, screaming their lungs out. The deafening roar of the water filled their ears as they plummeted down the seemingly endless drop. Taka's face contorted as he braced himself for the impact with the water.

The brothers crashed into the churning pool, and the raging falls submerged their bodies. Taka slammed into the sandy bottom, and Mufasa was tossed under a rock shelf.

Mufasa became motionless as his body plummeted under the surface of the water, his mind a tempest of thoughts and emotions. The last time he had been trapped underwater was that fateful day when he was a cub. Fear still clutched at his soul, and the weight of the water pressed down on him, the suffocating sensation all too familiar.

But then the force of the water shot them both back above the surface. They gasped for air until they found a floating fallen branch to grasp on to.

Kiros watched them from the island at the top of the waterfall, nodding as he saw them struggle. He grinned at how tenacious and foolish the two young lions were. He wouldn't make that dangerous jump to follow them; he ordered his hunters to find another quick way down.

Mufasa and Taka took one look at each other's drenched coats and broke out into fits of delirious laughter, fueled by adrenaline. They built off each other as they yelped in glee at escaping so narrowly.

"Mufasa, we're alive!" cried Taka. "I did it. I saved us."

Before Mufasa could reply, he caught sight of a looming figure emerging from under the water. The waterfall's dense mist made it difficult to discern the creature's features, but its size was undeniable—and as it grew closer, Mufasa knew for sure it was a white lion soldier.

"You were saying?" Mufasa asked Taka.

The white lion rose out of the mist and swam toward them with teeth bared, ready to strike.

Then, a flash of long green bodies! Crocodiles, with their jaws opened, emerged from the depths. They attacked the white lion from all sides, dragging it underwater in mere seconds.

The crocodiles approached Mufasa and Taka next,

with snapping jaws. Suddenly the raging waterfall severed in half the branch the brothers clung to—and the swirling current pushed them away from the action just in time.

Mufasa and Taka screamed as the churning waves carried them—until finally they emerged into shallow water.

"Okay. Okay," said Taka. "No more water."

∧∨∧∨∧

At the top of the falls, Kiros, Amara, and Akua stood on a plateau.

Kiros barked, "Tell me you can track them down the river."

Amara spewed out a laugh. "We can track them anywhere."

CHAPTER 10: BEFORE

After getting out of the shallow water, dripping wet, the young lions walked along, eventually finding their way into the woods. By the time night fell, their fur had dried and a massive grin had emerged on Taka's face.

"I did it agaaaiiiin," Taka sang. "I did it agaaaiinn. Not that I'm counting, but I saved your hide. Ah-gain. As much as it kills you to say it, let's hear a little 'thank you, Taka.'"

"Nope, not saying it," said Mufasa.

Taka hopped beside him. "I mean, okay, technically,

survived. As far as I can tell, a job well done."

Mufasa rolled his eyes. "Yeah, it was perfect other than nearly being crushed, drowned, and eaten."

Taka pushed him to the side lightly. "Look, it's not my fault crocodiles are simply attracted to you."

Mufasa sighed. "You tried to kill us. That's the opposite of saving."

His words got a smile out of Taka. This was familiar banter between the two of them.

"Wow . . . wow . . . how ungrateful," said Taka. "I did it agaiiinnn. I did it—" But he spotted something in the distance and stopped. "Mufasa."

Mufasa glanced at him once with widened eyes. "Shhh."

The dark night covered every inch of the Great Valley as the brothers crept toward a clearing. They heard a steady thump of footsteps. A herd of giant African buffalo passed in the distance. They settled at the clearing's edge.

Taka whispered, a paw to his belly, "Finally, food."

"First rule of hunting: be quiet," Mufasa told his brother. And though his stomach panged with hunger, he felt uneasy. "Something's wrong. The herds are moving away from the grasslands."

"So?" asked Taka.

"They're migrating the wrong way. I have to talk to them."

"Talk to the food?"

But before evaluating his brother's response, Mufasa moved toward the buffalo and shouted out: "Excuse me! Can I ask you a question? Hello—buffalo. My name is Mufasa...."

Several buffalo ignored him, continuing their marching, clearly unbothered by the sight of a lion. But the biggest of the group, with a broken horn, stepped out of the herd to meet Mufasa.

"We've heard of a lion named Mufasa," he said.

"You have?" cried Mufasa.

"The white lions came at us from the north," said the buffalo leader. "You defeated one, but you can't defeat an army."

Obasi's pride was not the only group of creatures in trouble, then.

"Where will you go?" Mufasa asked.

"To find a new home."

"We can fight them together!" Mufasa declared.

The buffalo, however, was uninterested. "You are a lion. There is no 'together.'"

The buffalo herd moved on, and Taka rejoined his brother.

"And there goes dinner," he said flatly.

"Taka—the balance is off," said Mufasa.

"Well, over the past day we've lost everyone and everything we've ever known and loved, so yes. It is."

"Taka," Mufasa said firmly. "We still have hope. We still have each other. And I promise you, I will get you to Milele. Help you build a new kingdom. Start a new legacy and preserve the bloodline."

Taka looked at him, silent for a few seconds before saying, "Our kingdom."

"What?" Mufasa asked.

Taka repeated, "Our kingdom. Wherever I am home, so are you, brother."

Mufasa's heart melted at his words, but before he could respond, something in the sky caught his attention. A bird flew in a practiced pattern over the buffalo herd and retreated into the woods. Mufasa sniffed the air.

"Is it them?" asked Taka. "Is it the white lions?"

Mufasa shook his head. "No . . . she's right there. . . ."

Taka raised his head. "She?"

They looked to their left, across the clearing, and a young female lion stared at them from the shadows. As Taka and Mufasa took a step forward, tiny branches crackling under their feet, the blinking eyes followed.

Mufasa broke the silence. "There's no place to run. We have your scent."

The lioness spoke from the dark. "My scent? I've been stalking you two all night."

"That's not possible," Mufasa said.

The lioness scoffed. "Then why did I just circle you three times in this wood while you were chasing each other's tails?"

Mufasa ran toward the lioness, sniffing the air. His suddenly uncoordinated gait made him crash into Taka. He nervously grinned and played it off like he'd meant to do that.

She snorted. "Still think I'm afraid?"

With this, she stepped out into the moonlight and walked toward them confidently, making eye contact.

"Why are you following us?" Mufasa asked.

She stopped short. "I was hoping to find my pride."

Mufasa lowered his guard a bit as he asked, "What happened to them?"

"The white lions happened," she replied. "A few of us got away, but . . . you're the only other lions I've seen. You two better keep moving."

She turned to go, but Taka followed her. "Wait! Wait! Please. My name is Taka—son of Obasi."

The lioness stopped as Taka slowly approached her. Mufasa looked on, a deep fold in his forehead.

"I know what it's like to lose everything," said Taka. "Come with us—we can help you."

She shook her head. "I don't need any help."

But Taka spoke in a whine, ears flattened atop his head. "But you don't have anyone."

Right at that moment, a bird came flying through the trees.

"She does indeed have someone, thank you very much!" the bird announced.

Taka, startled and alarmed, swiped at the bird, who jumped out of harm's way.

The lioness moved in front of the bird. "That's Zazu. Don't eat him."

"You heard her," Zazu said. "Do not eat me. As a recent addition to the king's royal guard, I must kindly ask you both to move on. Thank you for stopping by."

Taka stared at the pair with widened eyes before finally sputtering out, "Your king hired a bird to protect you?"

"They're not leaving," Zazu said to the lioness. "This is *awkward*."

She ignored the bird as she turned to Taka. "Tell me something, Taka: how high can you fly? Look, I needed a scout. Zazu was the last option."

Zazu ruffled his feathers. "Well, next to last. Between Albert the iguana and me, His Majesty decided on the underling with wings, and thus I became a lead scout for the princess. It's my third day, going swimmingly, if I may say so myself. Sarabi, you can say so as well."

Sarabi. So that was her name.

Mufasa listened to the conversation and then jumped in to say, "How far do you think you'll get with a bird?"

Sarabi rolled her eyes. "How far do you two geniuses think you'll get stumbling around talking to buffalo?"

Mufasa sauntered closer to her. "All the way to Milele."

Hearing this, Sarabi moved toward Mufasa. "Milele is nothing but a myth—"

"It's not a myth," Mufasa cut in.

Sarabi snorted. "A story told to cubs—you're chasing something that doesn't exist!"

She took a moment to truly regard him. But even under her intense stare, Mufasa did not back down.

"I don't know that Milele exists," he said, "but right now, it's the only hope we have."

"We don't need hope," she replied. "We need food."

Taka shook his head lightly at Mufasa. "Good job, brother. Oh, real nice."

The screeching sound of monkeys pierced the night, and the entire valley came alive. Taka stepped between Mufasa and Sarabi.

"Baboons . . ." said Taka.

Several of the creatures came into their view, perched above the lions' heads in trees that must have been over fifty feet tall.

Zazu peered around the lions. "There's trouble in the trees! My first real trouble and I'm going to pass. Not going. I'm staying right here."

Taka grinned widely. "Come on, Sarabi, looks like there's dinner headed our way!"

Mufasa and Taka bravely ran off in search of food, leaving Sarabi alone as she considered her options.

"Sarabi, if I may, there's a saying amongst the hornbills," said Zazu. "It doesn't matter how long you sit on a rock—it will never hatch."

"Zazu, what does that even mean?" she asked.

"I have no idea," admitted Zazu.

"*Zazu.*"

"Look," Zazu reasoned, "it can't be much worse, but... maybe it'll be... a little bit better."

Sarabi ran off, leaving Zazu behind.

"I think that went quite well, all things considered," Zazu said to himself.

CHAPTER 11: BEFORE

Hundreds of baboons swung their way through the trees, chattering and grooming each other as they went. A wild panic washed over the troop as they chased one younger monkey who didn't look quite like the others, until they cornered him at the end of a long branch.

"Order! We will have order in the congress of baboons!" one baboon elder announced.

His words were followed by silence as all three elders stepped forward.

The first elder spoke again, into the sudden hush.

"Tonight, a cheetah came into our trees for the third night in a row."

"Almost took one of our own," the second elder said.

"It was Rafiki's fault! He summoned the beast with his dreams," claimed the last elder.

The three elders pointed to the young creature the others had been chasing: Rafiki. The other baboons screeched their agreement.

"Rafiki and his visions must be banished once and for all," the first elder said.

The baboons moved to encircle Rafiki, but a female baboon named Junia jumped down from a branch to land in front of him.

"Rafiki tried to warn you!" she said.

"His dreams conjure our enemies!" the second elder retorted. "He talks to the spirits—summons the devil."

"What are you talking about?" asked Junia.

"He's done it before!" the third elder chimed in. "His brother was chased from these very trees, never to be seen again."

Junia scoffed. "Rafiki was just a child—"

"A child born with a leg that does not work," said the second elder. "Yet, somehow, he survived."

"It was Rafiki who found water in the dry season," Junia reminded them. "Who healed you, Inaki, when you were sick!"

"He speaks to the insects—converses with the moon," added the first elder.

"Zala, you know what will happen if you send him down from the trees," Junia warned.

"He is *amelaaniwa*," said the second elder, "a curse to us all! To his own brother!"

Junia shook her head. "No, that's not true...."

"He doesn't belong here," the third elder said. "All in favor of banishment—cover one eye."

One by one, each of the baboons covered one eye. With a sinking feeling, Rafiki realized his fate had been sealed.

"And so it is time," the young monkey said.

"Wait," said Junia. "Where will you go?"

Rafiki bolstered himself. "Where I should have gone long ago. To find all that was lost. My family."

"You can't survive on your own," Junia said sadly.

"Nobody can," Rafiki replied. "And yet, here we are."

He moved toward Junia and touched her brow with his hand.

"Rafiki . . ."

"The eye never forgets what the heart has seen," he told her.

As the baboons started reciting the chant of banishment together, Rafiki walked through the crowd and dropped from the massive tree—his hands grabbing branches as he swung his way down. He looked back at the others one last time before slowly disappearing beneath the cover of branches.

CHAPTER 12: NOW (INTERLUDE)

Kiara hated to be without her father and mother by her side, but she barely noticed the passage of time thanks to Rafiki's elaborate storytelling. Her eyes swelled with curiosity as Rafiki continued telling Mufasa's harrowing story. The drought, the deluge, the race, Milele, Rafiki's banishment, and more all held her attention.

Pumbaa and Timon also listened, breaking out into wails or songs as the story became sad, then cheerful, and then sad again.

"Spoiler alert! I know who Zazu is going to turn out to be," Pumbaa blurted out this time.

"It's Zazu," Kiara said plainly.

"Zazu is Zazu," Timon began, looking confusedly at Pumbaa. "Just like Pumbaa is Pumbaa. Understand?"

But Pumbaa didn't understand. Kiara and Timon just ignored him.

Rafiki then resumed his storytelling with a mischievous glimmer in his eyes. He continued recounting Mufasa's journey through the treacherous lands, describing his encounters with various animals and the challenges he faced along the way.

CHAPTER 13: BEFORE

ack in the Great Valley, Sarabi and Taka flanked Mufasa as the tall grass bit at their paws. They continued stealthily with eyes focused and ears perked, hunting for their next meal. They moved with purpose, their senses attuned to the surrounding wilderness. An obscured figure ambled up beside the clearing. With a nod from Sarabi, Mufasa leapt toward it and . . .

A young monkey appeared! He moved forward, staring directly into Mufasa's eyes, unfazed and disarming, and the two measured each other's strength. The creature's lack of fear momentarily stunned Mufasa, but then he shook himself out of it.

"You can try to run, but I'm afraid you won't get very far," Mufasa said.

"And why would I run from you?" the monkey said softly.

Sarabi and Taka stepped forward.

"Because we're lions," Taka said. "As in . . . lions!"

The monkey barked out a laugh. "A flea can trouble a lion more than a lion can trouble a flea."

He turned and walked away, uncaring of the other three. The lions turned to follow him.

Taka took another few steps to get closer to him. "I don't think you understand what's about to happen. There's no place for you to go."

"I am going forward," the monkey said without a waver in his voice.

"I seriously doubt that," Taka scoffed, puffing out his chest.

But the monkey walked along. "It is easy to doubt everything when you *know* nothing."

"Can we get on with this, please?" Sarabi cut in.

A fever rose up through Taka, and he stood ready to pounce on the monkey.

The creature stopped suddenly. "If you take my life, you will never find Milele."

Hearing the name of the place he wanted to find with all his being, Mufasa jumped between the monkey and Taka. "Wait. Did you say Milele?"

"That is where I am going—toward the light," the monkey said, his eyes glimmering with promise. "I've been there many times—in my dreams. My brother waits for me there. I have seen the tree—can picture it. The two of us together again."

Sarabi looked at the three of them and wondered aloud, "And why would anyone trust a baboon's dream?"

"Sometimes a dream is all you have," said the monkey. "The only truth that lives in you. Like the memory of a great king . . ."

"How did you know?" Sarabi asked, shocked.

Mufasa leaned closer, inches from the monkey, and

he said, "Okay, help us get to Milele—and we will let you live. Do we have a deal?"

"No," the monkey quickly snapped.

Mufasa flinched back. "What? Why?"

"Rafiki will let *you* live," he said, oddly speaking in the third person about himself.

Taka groaned loudly. "I've had enough of this."

Mufasa whirled around to him. "Taka—do not eat him!"

Sarabi scoffed as she stared at Mufasa with her mouth wide open. "Don't eat him? So you expect us to follow this baboon to a place nobody has ever seen? I'll be better off alone!"

Rafiki stepped toward Sarabi. "*Umdobasa*. If you wish to go fast, go alone. But if you wish to go far—go together."

With those words, he turned away. The three lions, standing silently in the wake of his wisdom, watched as he walked off.

Zazu swooped down with his wings spread wide,

casting a shadow over the lions as he landed with a heavy thud. As the lions stood dumbfounded, the bird gestured after Rafiki. "Okay, now that there's five of us, why don't we all go around and say a fun fact about ourselves? I'll go first: I once had a crush on a dodo." His voice dropped to a whisper. "I've never said that out loud."

Mufasa hesitated, torn between his desire to trust Rafiki's vivid imagination and his duty to protect his family. As Rafiki's shadow grew increasingly distant, his silhouette fading into the wilderness, Mufasa grappled with his choice. Should he trust this mysterious creature? Feeling the weight of his decision, Mufasa took a deep breath and started to follow Rafiki. Taka and Sarabi wordlessly joined him.

The group continued on, heading through the Great Valley, until they stopped at a small watering hole in the canyon for the night.

The three lions and Zazu huddled under the shelter of a rocky overhang, while Rafiki remained some distance away. As the night settled in, their breathing slowed and evened, indicating that they had finally drifted off to sleep.

After a while, Mufasa stirred, his mind too preoccupied to find rest. The weight of their journey ahead sat heavily on his mind, and he couldn't shake off his lingering doubts. He lay down on the rocky ground, gazing up at the starry sky, and took deep, calming breaths, trying to find some semblance of peace in the midst of his restless thoughts.

Gentle steps padded toward him. He craned his neck to see Sarabi coming to stand beside him. She got right over him, paw poised to lay atop his head.

Mufasa's gaze met Sarabi's. In that moment, captivated by her sheer beauty, he felt the extent of their differences: she, a lioness of noble lineage, destined for royalty; and he, a lion without that inherent birthright.

The realization tightened a knot within Mufasa's chest, stirring a sense of inadequacy. He turned away from Sarabi, breaking the connection they shared. He got up and stalked into the night, farther away from the group.

Rafiki sat by the pond on a rock facing the water—
with his eyes closed.

Mufasa stepped closer to him and whispered,
"Rafiki?"

"*Ey suga*," Rafiki called back.

"What are you doing?" Mufasa asked, squinting his
eyes.

"I am fishing," Rafiki replied.

"You're sitting on a rock with your eyes closed,"
Mufasa said, still confused.

"My eyes are open," Rafiki said, sounding old and
tired. "It is my lids that are closed."

Mufasa shook his head and wondered aloud, "Why
am I talking to a baboon?"

"I am not a baboon," Rafiki declared. "I am a
mandrill."

"A what?" Mufasa said.

"Rafiki was born a mandrill," Rafiki began, oddly
referencing himself in the third person again. "But not
born alone. There was a brother who knew the beat of my
mother's heart. . . ."

"A twin?" Mufasa asked with a lilt in his voice.

"Mandrills fear all twins," Rafiki began. "Believe we see the unseeable—speak the unspeakable! And so the two were abandoned in the trees—left to die. Until the baboons raised us as their own."

When Mufasa heard this, he said, "No offense, but a monkey is a monkey."

"And a stray is a stray," Rafiki said, firing back.

Mufasa gritted his teeth. "What's that supposed to mean?"

"It means we are very much the same," Rafiki said, comparing how both of them had lost their kindred. "*Cee afona.*"

Mufasa hesitated but then said, "I am not a twin."

"And I am not a baboon!" Rafiki retorted.

"We are nothing alike!" Mufasa said, nearly yelling. "Take a good look: I am a lion!"

"A lion who fears the water," Rafiki said. "Fears his own reflection. Who can't sleep because of what he sees when he closes his eyes."

Mufasa's forehead furrowed. "Huh?"

"You are afraid of your *dreams*, Mufasa," Rafiki continued, looking keenly into Mufasa's eyes. "Afraid of what you see in them."

"I see him," Mufasa said. "The white lion. I feel his hatred."

"But *why* does he hate *you*?" Rafiki asked.

Mufasa stared at his paws, the ones he'd used to commit a horrible act. "He hates me . . . because I killed his son."

"No, he hates you because he wants his son," Rafiki said.

"His son is gone," Mufasa said.

Rafiki nodded. "Yes, but soon a son will find *him*."

Rafiki plunged his hand inside the pond and pulled out a large fish. It flapped and flailed in Rafiki's outstretched hands. He observed the fish with extreme attention to detail and turned it around in his hands for a while as he came eye to eye with it. He whispered words unknown to Mufasa as he returned the fish to the pond, seemingly casting a spell: *"Ni heshima kukutana nawe, binamu. Nenda kwa amani."*

Mufasa stared at him, his eyes wide. "What are you doing? We're starving."

"It was not its time. Instead, the fish has agreed to let us share the water," Rafiki said calmly.

Within moments, Rafiki jumped into the pond and waded through the water, making the surface ripple as he passed. He whispered: *"Ek a Rafiki. Ek a clasemon. Ummm."*

From the edge of the pond, Mufasa watched Rafiki's antics with curiosity.

As the first rays of sunlight spread across the horizon, nearly on cue Zazu flew in to join them. The hornbill flapped his wings for a soft landing at Mufasa's feet, and Mufasa jumped back.

His feathers tousled by the wind, Zazu blurted out, "I have a report." He paused. "It's morning. End of report."

One thing was clear: they needed to decide what path

to take. Mufasa called out to Sarabi and Taka, and they sprang up from under the rocky overhang to gather with the others. Rafiki emerged from the water to join in, too. Another day of travel lay ahead.

CHAPTER 14: BEFORE

Together, the gang ran through rays of the sun, the savannah floor brightening by the minute. They reached the valley ridge, peering down into the canyon in this serrated terrain.

Rafiki walked a few steps ahead. "The earth divided is now a choice. Around or down. The decision is yours."

Mufasa stood at the edge of the cliff, his gaze fixated on the jagged rocks below. How could they possibly navigate the treacherous terrain to reach Milele? The burden of the decision weighed heavily on him, and his eyes darted across the landscape, searching for any clues for how to get across—and then he remembered Eshe's words.

"Across the deepest canyon . . ." he recalled. "We should go down."

Sarabi stepped forward. "Why, because of some fairy tale?"

"The rocks will hide our tracks," he said.

"It's safer to go around!" Sarabi proposed.

"I've picked up their scent," Mufasa argued.

"The only thing you picked up is a hallucinating baboon!" she said. She turned to Rafiki. "No offense."

"Close your eyes," Mufasa whispered, moving closer to her.

Sarabi's eyes widened. "What?"

Mufasa started to repeat himself, but Taka interrupted: "This is a waste of time. . . ."

Taka stared at Sarabi, who hesitated . . . but then did as Mufasa asked.

Mufasa edged in her direction, "Tell me what you see. What you feel."

Sarabi sniffed the air. She lifted her head, trying to catch every scent. "There's nothing on the wind."

Mufasa rocked forward. "No. They're moving through the bush willow."

Sarabi, eyes still closed said, "They who?"

"The females. Out front," Mufasa said. "Come on. Clear your thoughts. Concentrate."

Her forehead scrunched up. "I am concentrating." An image as clear as the blue sky flashed behind her eyelids. It was the white lions charging toward them. Then her eyes opened wide suddenly in disbelief. "He's right. We have to go down."

Rafiki, who watched all this happen from his own perch at the edge, smiled and spoke his approval: "Aye twende."

Sarabi pushed past them as she bounded into the canyon, leading the way. Mufasa turned to follow but looked at Taka standing still. "Come on, Taka."

Taka eyed his brother. Then his gaze landed on Sarabi's retreating form. Standing alone, he lifted his head to sniff the wind, "Hmmm . . . bush willow."

Although he tried, no scent reached him. No matter what, he could not be as talented as Mufasa or Sarabi.

The gang ventured forward into the canyon, descending as Zazu soared above them. They made their way through the winding path of the Great Canyon, and the towering walls rose up beside them, reaching an intimidating height. Undeterred by the rugged terrain, they pressed forward with determination, while Zazu kept a watchful eye from above, focused on identifying any dangers that lay ahead.

"Okay, Zazu," he began, talking to himself. "Have confidence in your abilities. The gang has nothing but respect for you. Remember that. Well, they haven't eaten you yet. That's for starters. All you have to do is just remain uneaten. That's the key to the job. As long as you're not their dinner. You are a valued member of the gang."

Zazu maintained his watch as the group moved through the canyon—until the sun began to set. Taka leaned against a canyon wall, his breaths labored as he complained about the heat. He asked for water or something to offer him some nourishment. His paws, like the others', were scratched and ached from having trekked all day long.

"Water?" Sarabi scoffed. "Down here? Good luck with that."

Mufasa yelped beside them. "Guys, we have to focus!"

"Focus on what exactly? There's nothing here," Taka said, looking around with exhausted eyes.

Sarabi glanced between the two brothers. "No, Taka, there's plenty here. Just ask Mufasa."

Mufasa considered Taka's weakened posture, then sighed. "Zazu will find us water." He yelled up at the circling bird. "Right, Zazu?"

Zazu yelled back, "Whatever you say, Captain!" As he took off, he muttered to himself, "How on earth am I supposed to find *water* . . . out *here?*"

Rafiki sat on a jagged rock, watching the frustrated group with a keen eye. The gang trudged a bit farther through the canyon until Mufasa halted suddenly, the others loping past him. His sharp eyes had picked out a diverging path, camouflaged among the rocks and sand.

"Guys, wait," he called out, scurrying farther away. "There's a path here. It's a sign."

Begrudgingly, the group followed his lead. Off the main path, they moved single file through the slender hidden corridor, their footsteps echoing off the canyon walls. Mufasa barreled ahead, snaking his way through the narrow passage.

Eventually, though, they reached a dead end: canyon walls still rose up around them, a sheer and impenetrable barrier. The group scanned their surroundings in disbelief. The ground was rough and uneven, and the only thing in sight was a solitary gnarled tree with a pile of wrinkled fruit at its base.

Sarabi sniffed the fruit. "See what listening to your little fairy tale got us? A dead end and rotten fruit." She moved away from them, over to the sheer face of the cul-de-sac. "Look, if we're careful, I think we can scale our way back up to the rim right here."

"What?" Mufasa asked as he moved closer to her. "I thought we agreed we're better off in the canyon."

Sarabi sighed. "Yeah, well, now we don't. I'm getting out of here."

Taka spoke up behind them. "But, Sarabi, you can't just leave."

"Watch me," Sarabi said, rolling her eyes.

Taka sprinted ahead and nudged Mufasa. "Mufasa! Do something!"

Mufasa turned away. "Let her go. There's nothing up there but white lions and a bowl of sand. It's Zazu's fault."

Zazu, circling around the group at a low height, landed on one of the tree branches. "My fault?"

Mufasa looked up at him. "Yeah, what kind of scout flies around an entire day and can't find water!"

"Yeah, well it's not all roses having wings, you know!" Zazu said, flapping. "I deserve a bit of grace!"

Taka squinted. "You know what—why don't we just eat him?"

"As if!" Zazu scoffed.

"Taka!" Mufasa admonished.

A shouting match broke out among them, each one going for another's throat. The argument had reached a fever pitch when an unexpected sound pierced the air, silencing them all. A howling Rafiki sat among the pile of marula fruit. The three lions and the hornbill stared at the confusing mandrill.

"Rafiki, are you . . . okay?" Mufasa asked.

Rafiki harrumphed. "Me? Of course I am okay! I am eating the fruit provided by this generous tree."

Sarabi side-eyed him. "Yeah, but look at it. That can't be good for you."

A woozy smile crossed Rafiki's face. He rolled a few balls of marula toward the gang. They tumbled to the feet of Mufasa, Taka, and Sarabi, who looked down suspiciously at the wrinkled fruit. Zazu poked his head up from between the surrounding marulas, examining them carefully with his long beak.

"Would Rafiki eat it if it wasn't good for Rafiki?" the mandrill asked, letting out a big, spirited laugh before he chomped into the juicy fruit.

First Mufasa, then the others also began to eat the fruit, realizing it was harmless, as Rafiki had said. The juice rolled down their cheeks. They licked themselves clean and purred in delight.

"Mmmmhmmm, this will make you feel much better now," said Rafiki. "Come on, we have places to go."

"And people to see!" added Zazu.

Rafiki laughed and gestured for the group to follow him. His steady gait eased into a jaunty side step as he began to sing. Sarabi joined in, and then the others did, too. The melody encouraged them to keep their hopes up and stick together.

Seeing Sarabi's face brighten inspired Taka. But he couldn't bear to let her know how his feelings for her were developing. It would cause too much disruption. He masked his longing with a friendly smile.

After their spirits had all been lifted, the group became even more resolved to stick together. But at the end of the day, they fell into a fitful sleep.

CHAPTER 15: BEFORE

ack in the Great Valley, the white lions exited the tall grasses and entered a clearing. The hunters kept their noses to the air, tracking Mufasa and the gang's every move. They could tell the group had only recently been here.

Amara's ears stood straight up. "Kiros . . . they're not alone."

"They've collected a lioness," said Akua.

"And a monkey," Amara added.

The white lions walked forward, and Kiros sensed something staring down at them from high above in the trees. Kiros climbed up a tree, higher and higher until he reached a thick landing. He took a moment to scan the canopy—and came face to face with a sea of terrified baboons looking back at him silently with bated breath.

The baboon Junia slowly lowered herself behind him.

"The one of your tribe recently departed, who is he?" Kiros said to the baboons in front of him, his tone commanding a response.

"He's not of this tribe!" a baboon elder boomed, trying to appear brave. "He and his dark magic were a curse upon us all."

"There is no magic, only might," Kiros scoffed. "He travels with lions now. Do you know where they are going?"

"What could we know about a journey we are not taking?" Junia interjected, offering a contrarian perspective. She'd always been interested in protecting Rafiki. The others, it seemed, still felt no loyalty toward him.

But then a new voice emerged—another baboon elder. "Milele."

"Rafiki believes he is the prophet who will find Milele," another baboon bemoaned.

"He knows when the earth will shake," a third said.

Kiros listened to this information quietly before he leapt off the landing and strolled to the edge of the canyon, eyeing the horizon ahead. His son's murderer wandered somewhere out there among the plains, and he was destined to bring him to justice.

CHAPTER 16: NOW (INTERLUDE)

Timon's eyes widened at Rafiki. "Wait, wait, wait, so—now you're the star of this thing?"

"All of a sudden there's a lot of Rafiki in this story," Pumbaa added.

"You even gave yourself a long-lost brother!" said Timon. "What's next, a funny catchphrase?"

Kiara, disinterested in Timon and Pumbaa's banter, chased a firefly. The firefly's tiny glow danced in the air, leading her away from the group.

Rafiki moved up onto a platform beside them to get a better view of Kiara. "You cannot tell the story of Mufasa—without the story of Rafiki."

Kiara whispered in the wind, "Mom—if you can hear me. Come home. Please . . . come home. . . ."

She closed her eyes, hoping that her words would float off and reach her mom, wherever she was.

CHAPTER 17: BEFORE

Mufasa and the gang made their way through the Great Canyon. Sarabi and Rafiki took the lead, allowing Taka and Mufasa to hang back.

Taka turned to his brother. "Mufasa, Mufasa—you have to help me."

"Help you how?" Mufasa asked.

Taka hummed low in his throat. "You were right. As you said, there are brighter days ahead. It's Sarabi, Mufasa. She is the light my mother spoke of."

"What?" Mufasa asked, looking puzzled.

Taka whisper-shouted, "She's special, the most

amazing female I've ever met in my life. I don't know what to say to her! You've spent your whole life with females. Please—tell me what to say."

"Why do you need *me*?" Mufasa huffed. "Just . . . talk to her. Be yourself."

"No, Mufasa, you don't understand—myself isn't good enough," Taka said, shaking his head. "You . . . just know things. She needs to see me . . . more like you."

Mufasa stopped walking, startled by Taka's admission. Mufasa couldn't help feeling a twinge of conflict. Sarabi had begun to hold a special place in his heart since that night under the rocky overhang, and though he knew he was a mere stray while she was a princess, he'd hoped to get to know her better. Yet here he was, faced with the knowledge that his own brother felt the same way. His brother, who held the royal blood of the pride.

He swallowed his feelings and tried to be helpful to Taka. "Fine. Fine. Keep it simple. Ask her a question."

"Right!" Taka nodded. "A question. This is good."

"Yeah, try to be confident—disinterested," Mufasa replied.

Taka squinted at his advice. "But I'm very interested!"

Mufasa paused, realizing that he really didn't know what was the best thing to say. He spoke the next thought that came to him. "Tell her about the flowers."

"What flowers?"

"The valley she comes from—there are flowers everywhere," Mufasa explained. "They're called duck flowers. Long stems. It's absolutely beautiful."

"How do you know that?" Taka asked.

Mufasa looked up at Sarabi, who walked ahead of them. "When she passes, I can smell them on her fur."

He understood the significance of Sarabi's presence, recognizing her as a remarkable lioness. No wonder both he and Taka wanted to know her better.

"Okay," Taka said. "Flowers. Disinterested."

"And here's the most important thing, okay?" Mufasa added. "Listen when she speaks."

Taka remained in his own head as he stared ahead blankly, mumbling to himself. "Flowers. Disinterested."

Mufasa continued, nearly under his breath, "Males have trouble with that one."

"Sorry, what did you say?" Taka asked.

Sarabi strode ahead, her gait purposeful as she walked through vertical columns rising out of the canyon bed. The relentless sun beat down upon the group, adding to their discomfort. Taka bounded up beside her but made no eye contact with her.

"It's very hot, isn't it?" he finally asked.

Sarabi looked at him without any obvious expression on her face. "Yup."

She kept on walking without another word.

Taka tried again. "I . . . love listening."

"Okaaaay," Sarabi said.

Taka kept on going. "I'm listening right now."

"To what?" Sarabi asked.

"What you just said," Taka replied.

Sarabi turned toward him with one of her brows raised. "You're the one that's talking."

"I am." Taka laughed awkwardly. "You smell like a duck."

"What?" Sarabi asked, frowning.

"Flower," Taka corrected. "A duck flower—"

Sarabi gasped. "How do you know about those flowers?"

Taking a cue from Mufasa, Taka replied, "Well, I inhaled you with my nose. I can smell them. . . ."

Sarabi flexed her ears. "That's amazing. Our valley was full of those flowers—thousands of them as far as the eye could see. It was the most beautiful place, Taka."

Taka purred low in his throat. "Well, every time I see those flowers, it will remind me of you."

Sarabi bowed her head. "Thank you for reminding me of home."

Taka hummed, happy that he finally talked with Sarabi on his own. "We all need that sometimes."

They walked quietly for a few moments, then Taka said, "Sarabi . . . thank you for talking to me."

Sarabi looked at him again, confused. "Why wouldn't I talk to you?"

"As prince, no one ever really talks to me. Except Mufasa," Taka said, facing the ground. "It's just nice. Thank you."

The sun beat down on the group as they trudged through the arid canyon, their once lively strides reduced to heavy, labored steps. Their parched throats ached for water, and though the juicy marula fruit they had eaten earlier had helped, it was not enough. Their weary eyes scanned the surrounding terrain for any sign of relief from the scorching heat, but the ground was only littered with spiky rock columns that became denser the farther they went, providing even more obstacles to their passage.

A bee darted over Mufasa's head and past Sarabi's ear, and they watched as it flew toward another fork in their path. The left side contained a pileup of those jagged, spiky rocks, but on the right side, a ramp of rocks jolted up out of the canyon. Rafiki stopped to gaze at the two pathways.

Mufasa's senses were on high alert. A tremor brushed his fur, a subtle vibration, his senses picking up on the sound of something approaching. He sniffed the air, and his nostrils flared and his ears twitched as he tried to identify the source of the noise. As the rumbling grew louder, Taka and Sarabi joined him, their eyes scanning the horizon for any sign of danger.

Then, with a ground-shaking tremor, a colossal herd of elephants materialized on the distant savannah, a massive procession stretching as far as the eye could see. Like a harmonious symphony, the earth trembled beneath the synchronized footsteps of these majestic creatures, whose trunks swung rhythmically as they marched across the vast expanse.

A sense of awe and wonder washed over Mufasa as the herd passed by. The elephants moved with grace and power, but this beautiful and intimidating force blocked the gang's path forward.

Taka jumped back, astonished. "A gray wall. Mufasa, we've walked into a . . . a gray wall."

"They shouldn't be here," said Mufasa. "The migration patterns are broken. I don't understand this."

Zazu swooped in then, shouting: "WHITE LIONS!

THIS IS NOT A DRILL! JUST TO BE CLEAR I NEVER SIGNED UP FOR THIS!"

Zazu was right: in the distance, Kiros and his army kicked up dust as they made their way along the far rim of the canyon. One of them casually hopped from the rim onto the first of the three rock columns lining the expanse, growing ever closer to Mufasa's group.

Taka's breath picked up. "They can just jump across—we're trapped. What do we do?"

Mufasa needed to come up with a plan—and fast!

CHAPTER 18: BEFORE

Mufasa's eyes moved between the elephants and the white lions approaching, and something clicked in his mind.

"The elephants will fight with us!" he said.

Sarabi's eyes widened with disbelief. "And why would they do that?"

"Because—I'm going to ask them," said Mufasa. "Have a better idea?"

"Yes, Mr. Ask Questions First," she retorted. She took off, shouting, "Get ready to run!"

Sarabi jumped down into a jagged crevice and charged toward the line of elephants.

"Where is she going?" Taka shouted.

One of the white lions appeared in their line of vision, across the canyon rim. They had to move quickly, and surely, the only way forward was through the gray wall. Taka followed Sarabi, jumping after her into the same crevice.

Mufasa took a different path but landed near the elephant herd. As Mufasa drew closer, the ground shook beneath his feet and he struggled to maintain his balance. The trumpeting of the elephants grew louder, and their massive bodies seemed to fill his entire vision.

"Hello?" Mufasa called up to them. "Listen to me, please, we need your help. Can you talk with me? We need your help. Please."

But despite their imposing presence, the elephants trumpeted him away, and they continued on, trampling over anything in their path.

Mufasa felt a pang of disappointment; his attempt to get the elephants' help was in vain. But he couldn't stop now. He could see a white lion hunting him, tracking his movements among the elephant herd. Turning the other way, he saw Sarabi emerging at the base of a tree on the far side of the herd.

Zazu's sharp eyes had picked up something else on the horizon. "They're coming!"

Taka continued to follow Sarabi. "Sarabi! Sarabi, wait! Sarabi, wait!"

Spotting something dangling off a tree branch ahead, Sarabi had formed an idea. She wove through the elephants' legs until she reached the tree, then climbed up before charging across a long branch toward the thing that had caught her eye.

Rafiki intently followed her moves with his eyes and realized her plan. "She's going for the hive!"

Just after making eye contact with Mufasa, Sarabi screamed, "Like I said—get ready to run!"

She swatted at the hive until it toppled down from the branches, sailed over the gray wall of elephants, and split open on the savannah floor. In a flash, a cloud of bees buzzed out and zoomed around the herd of elephants.

Caught off guard by the sudden onslaught of bees, the elephants erupted into a frenzy of panic and chaos, running in every direction. Their massive bodies convulsed, ears flapping madly as the bees buzzed relentlessly, stinging wherever they could. One bee even went inside an elephant's trunk. In their attempts to escape, the elephants tripped over one another, causing even more shrieking and trumpeting.

Rafiki said at the top of his lungs, "Get to the trees!"

He began to run, and so did Zazu, who quickly exclaimed, "Why am I running?" before taking off into the sky. Taka was still stuck in a nearby crevice, waiting for his chance to escape.

Rafiki climbed up into the nearest tree and perched on its branches to scan the melee below. He saw Mufasa, ducking and weaving through the rampaging elephants, still stuck in the middle of the chaos as two white lions stalked him.

One white lion also dodged the elephants and caught up with Mufasa. The white lion licked his chops and roared, ready to pounce on his prey.

Thwack!

The noise resounded throughout the canyon as an

elephant rammed into the white lion and the lion fell limply to the ground. Mufasa sighed at his luck, but then came another *thwack* as a different elephant bumped into him. His body sailed through the air before crashing against the side of a thick tree trunk.

As Mufasa regained his bearings and woozily scrambled up the tree, Sarabi was still clinging to her own long branch—but her grip was loosening as the limb bobbed in the wake of the elephants' thunderous stampede.

"Your Highness!" Zazu shouted from above. "Hold on!"

"Zazu!" Sarabi wailed.

He dove down to save her, but he was too late. Sarabi slipped and fell toward the dusty ground. Her head slammed into the thick, hardened roots at the base of the tree, and she lay motionless as more elephants headed toward her.

Mufasa cried out, his voice hoarse: "Sarabi!"

He jumped down from his position on the tree trunk and leapt between the elephants, running between massive legs and feet, desperately trying to reach her. He avoided a collision with one huge elephant as another barreled toward him.

Taka watched from the crevice where he hid. He took a step forward, but the desire to help his friends, to contribute his strength and bravery, warred with his overwhelming fear. Doubt gnawed at his resolve, and he became paralyzed with indecision.

Meanwhile, Mufasa reached Sarabi, his breath choppy from skirting countless elephants. He dragged her a few feet across the flat surface and down into a jagged fault carved into the land. He shielded her with his body and the tree while elephants pushed past them. The ground shook, and he could barely see with all of the kicked-up dirt.

Mufasa whispered, nearly crying, "I got you! I got you! Sarabi, I got you!"

The white lions stopped dead in their tracks. The ground shook as a cloud of dust revealed elephants running straight at them. With no choice but to jump back to the other side of the canyon, they sprinted for their lives across the rock bridge they'd come from.

The elephants charged over the side and down into the canyon. Some slid and rolled as they slammed into the base of a center column, which buckled from their force. The bridge collapsed, rocks and dust exploding in its wake, and the white lions remaining on top fell as the pillar of rocks crashed down, too. The white lions who'd escaped clung to the far rim of the canyon, now cut off from pursuing Mufasa and the others.

Kiros looked skyward and locked eyes with the gliding scout, Zazu. His patience dwindled, and a feverish anger rose from his body. He summoned a mighty roar that echoed across the savannah.

Everything turned quiet after the white lions, elephants, and bees had fled. The entire area looked like a storm had hit it—roots and rocks and branches everywhere, and dust floating in the air.

As the dust finally settled, Rafiki clung to a high tree branch.

"Thank you, my friend," he said to the branch.

With a snap, the branch broke, and Rafiki dropped to the ground, landing in a pile of tree limbs—a bit bruised, but alive. He crawled out of the pile, the branch he'd clung to still in his hand. This branch would make an excellent walking stick.

Rafiki looked out to see where Mufasa and Sarabi might be.

"Over here!" came Mufasa's voice from a nearby crevice, covered in debris.

After a few tense moments, Taka emerged from his hiding spot and moved toward the crevice, his head hanging in shame.

When he saw that his brother and Sarabi were trapped, his heart panged.

He steeled himself, ran toward them, and assisted Rafiki in clearing away the debris that had covered Mufasa and Sarabi. Once free, Mufasa slowly got to his feet, shaken but alive.

Taka was relieved to see Mufasa safe and sound, but looking down at the unconscious Sarabi, his heart caught in his throat. He remembered the feeling of abandoning his mother to the white lions' attack at the Shade Tree. It became difficult for him to breathe.

He'd done it again—run away instead of standing his ground and fighting, like Mufasa had. First he'd been unable to protect his mother, and now Sarabi. Why hadn't he grown from his past mistakes?

But he knew why: he would never be as brave as Mufasa. It had been written in stone; nothing could be done about it.

Meanwhile, as Taka stewed in sorrow, Mufasa still watched over Sarabi. He'd done his best to save her, but had it been enough? He couldn't imagine continuing on this journey without her.

Someone came up next to him. His rigid form relaxed when he recognized the presence of Rafiki.

With a glint in his eyes, Rafiki leaned down to Sarabi's level, cupped her face in his hands, and blew into it. He said a spell aloud: "*Vuta Pumzi. Sarabi . . .*"

Rafiki blew several times again . . . until Sarabi started to choke and cough, finally able to take a deep breath.

"Alive," said Rafiki. "She's alive."

Sarabi opened her eyes and blinked a few times to

clear her blurred vision. Then she stared up at her companions and quickly got to her feet, her tail swishing behind her as if she was ready for another fight. Seeing no immediate threat in her vicinity, nor hearing the sound of elephants running, she relaxed—though the gang all stared at her in silence.

"Why are you all looking at me?" she asked.

"You were thrown from the tree," Rafiki said. "He saved your life."

"Who?"

Mufasa stepped forward timidly.

In that moment, as Mufasa noticed Taka with his head bowed in shame, a decision rippled through his mind—a decision to shield Taka from the truth, to weave a protective cocoon around him that would temporarily alleviate his guilt and preserve the bond between them.

He shook his head. "Taka. Taka saved you. Isn't that right, brother?"

Everyone turned their heads to Taka. His brain went blank, caught off guard by the sudden rewriting of what had happened.

"You saved me?" Sarabi asked Taka.

"Well...I...had to do something," Taka stammered, his lies squeezing through his teeth. The chance to be remembered as honorable and valiant proved more appetizing than telling the truth.

Sarabi bowed her head at Taka. "Thank you."

"We're lucky," said Mufasa. "Those bees almost killed us all."

"Those bees saved our lives," she retorted. She knew that her quick thinking had truly been their saving grace.

"Really?" said Mufasa. "Because it felt like an elephant stampede!"

Taka observed their interaction and grew despondent again. He saw the way Mufasa and Sarabi looked at each other, and the ease with which their interactions flowed, and he felt like an outsider. He didn't relate as effortlessly to Sarabi as Mufasa did, and a bout of loneliness welled inside of him.

"We're alive, aren't we?" Sarabi argued.

"The elephants would have fought with us!" Mufasa insisted.

"We're lions!" said Sarabi. "Nobody will fight with us. Not out here."

Rafiki burst into an upbeat song, interrupting the argument. He continued to sing and whistle as he walked away. The group, still reeling from the disarray caused by the elephants and white lions, stared at him, their jaws slack.

"Where is he going?" asked Sarabi.

Mufasa recognized one lyric of the song: Milele.

"Beyond the horizon itself," said Mufasa.

They followed him, though, because they could only move forward.

"**R**afiki, who are the white lions?" Kiara asked, interrupting the story. She sat on the edge of a watering hole within the cave.

"The white lions come from many prides," Rafiki said. "But when they are born, they are hated because they are different from their tribe."

"Like you and your tribe?" Kiara asked.

"Yes. Just like me," Rafiki said matter-of-factly.

"But Rafiki . . ." Kiara began.

"Yes?"

"Why do they want to hurt everybody?"

"Sometimes, when the people most like you don't love you, it is a hurt that can cause the greatest pain. And this pain can lead you to hate . . . everything."

Kiara paused, then said, "I am glad that didn't happen to you, Rafiki."

Her sweet voice warmed Rafiki's heart. "Yes, my child. I'm glad, too."

He pulled Kiara into a comforting hug.

CHAPTER 20: BEFORE

ufasa realized they'd stumbled into uncharted territory, where muted ash from a dormant volcano lay in the distance, covering the expanse.

Taka walked ahead with Sarabi, and Mufasa purposefully trailed behind them. Now that Mufasa knew of Taka's affection for Sarabi, he wanted nothing more than to see his brother happy. So Mufasa decided to nudge fate in the direction of their budding romance, even as his heart wrestled over whether he was doing the right thing.

Rafiki sidled up next to Mufasa, bemused. "A giraffe with two tongues chokes on a single leaf."

Mufasa had quickly become used to Rafiki's odd murmurings. At night, Rafiki sat on the tallest rock and meditated, always keeping a close eye on their surroundings.

Mufasa broke his gaze away from Taka and Sarabi. "What's that supposed to mean?"

"You tell me," Rafiki said.

Mufasa stared at him, brows raised. "So now I'm a giraffe?"

Rafiki shook his head slowly. "No, you are the camel."

Mufasa snorted. "A camel?"

Rafiki nodded. "A camel does not see his own hump."

"If I had a hump, I would see it!" Mufasa grunted. "But I don't. So . . . not a camel."

This time, Rafiki turned to him, his brows raised. "And why did you lie to Sarabi?"

Mufasa stared at the ground. "I made a promise to take care of my brother—to save my pride, I . . ."

His voice trailed off. He wanted to convince Rafiki, but the way Rafiki looked at him made it obvious that he might be trying to convince himself. In hindsight, he did not know why he'd said that Taka had saved Sarabi. The lie had just rolled out of him so easily. Maybe, somewhere in the recesses of his mind, guilt was growing over the way he felt about all of it, but more specifically Sarabi.

When Mufasa did not say anything further, Rafiki said, "Mufasa, no matter how far you walk, destiny will follow."

With that, he walked off, leaving Mufasa behind. Mufasa stood motionless, lost in his own thoughts. He regretted lying to Sarabi; he knew it didn't feel entirely right, but he couldn't help himself. Why did he feel obligated to make Taka look braver than he was? He loved his brother and wanted him to overcome his struggles with self-doubt and insecurity. This would be necessary if Taka hoped to become the future king.

He stared at a large, powerful shadow on the nearby wall and startled when he realized that it was, in fact, his own. He possessed the strength, wisdom, and potential to become a leader in his own right. The realization both exhilarated and unnerved him, as it presented a crucial question: Would stepping up to fulfill his destiny as a leader be seen as a betrayal of his beloved brother?

The sound of falling rocks jolted him out of his reverie, and the sudden noise caused Mufasa's fur to stand on end. The silt from the rim of the crater cascaded down the chasm, creating a miniature rockslide. He looked up to see the debris bouncing down the cliff face and disappearing into the depths below.

Mufasa couldn't help wondering if the rockslide was some kind of omen—a warning from the universe to stop lying and start being honest with himself and others. Was he meant to step up and lead after all?

He shook his head to clear the cobwebs from his mind, and he resolved to be more truthful from that moment on.

＊＊＊

The gang continued along the barren plateau. As they walked through the rocky terrain, they couldn't help feeling overwhelmed by the sheer magnitude of the formations surrounding them. The stone pillars towered above them while sculptures of rock seemed to twist and turn in every direction. It was as if they had entered a different world, one that was both beautiful and unforgiving.

As they pressed on, their eyes fixed on the horizon, the rocky landscape slowly gave way to something even more stunning—snow-capped mountains rising up like giant sentinels in the distance. The gang's jaws dropped in awe as they took in the majestic peaks that loomed before them. In the beautiful glow of sunset, the mountains seemed to stretch on endlessly, their snowy peaks disappearing into the clouds above.

With each step they took, the air grew colder, and soon the gang shivered in the biting wind, their breath coming out in visible puffs. They huddled closer together, trying to conserve their heat as they left the mountain basin and climbed up a slight incline.

∧∨∧∨∧

Meanwhile, as night fell, the white lions charged forward through the desert in hot pursuit of their prey. The moon hung low in the sky, casting an eerie glow over the land.

Kiros's breath came in ragged gasps, but he refused to let his exhaustion take over.

At the rear of the group, one lion slowed and then collapsed, right near the edge of a grand crater. The others stopped to gauge the lion's condition, but Kiros only regarded him coldly. He could just as easily leave behind anyone too weak for the journey.

The lion seemed to get the message and stumbled to his feet. The group ran past Kiros, continuing their relentless search.

But just as Kiros made to follow, he noticed his own shadow cast in the crater—and then smelled something in the air, a scent that was tantalizingly close, yet just out of reach. It was a scent that he knew all too well.

⌃⌄⌃⌄⌃

Even as the moon twinkled in the sky, Mufasa's group continued moving ahead through the mountains, their paws aching with every step. The weight of their exhaustion settled on their shoulders as they finally reached a clearing. They scanned the area for any sign of danger before settling down to rest for the night. One by one, their eyes began to droop and they drifted off into a deep slumber.

After a couple of hours of sleep, Mufasa sprang to life, eyes alert and chest heaving from a nightmare. The cold settled into his bones and he shivered. Mufasa shook off the snow and looked around him. Had anyone else felt this sudden foreboding chill, beyond the cold itself? But Taka, Sarabi, and Zazu remained fast asleep.

Only Rafiki stayed awake. He sat nearby on a ridge, watching Mufasa as though waiting for him.

Mufasa hiked up to the little perch but did not say anything about his abrupt awakening.

"*Ek Rafiki. Ek sielsmana,*" Rafiki said.

As Mufasa approached, the words became clearer, but he still didn't understand. "Hey, Rafiki, what are you doing?"

"I am . . . confirming my vision, Mufasa."

Mufasa settled down beside him. "Can I ask you something, Rafiki?"

"Hmmm."

"How many of your visions have come true?" Mufasa asked with a curious lilt.

"So far? None," Rafiki said plainly.

"None," Mufasa repeated, anxiety welling from his paws to his face.

"But it's not what I see, it's what I feel," Rafiki emphasized.

"But how do you . . . how do you know when you should follow a feeling?" Mufasa said, still unnerved.

"Milele exists," Rafiki said sharply. "I feel it. In *here*. The question is, what do you feel, Mufasa? In *there*?"

Rafiki pointed to Mufasa's chest while locking eyes with the young lion.

After his conversation with Rafiki, Mufasa returned to his resting spot and fell back asleep for a while longer. When morning broke, the group groggily awoke, shivering from the cold and trying to shake off the snow that had settled on their fur overnight. Sarabi yawned loudly, stretching her limbs to get her blood flowing again. Taka rubbed his eyes, trying to get rid of the sleep that still clung to him.

They continued on their journey, and the snowfall grew heavier, turning the landscape into a swirl of white. Mufasa trudged ahead of them, breaking through the snow and forging a path for the rest of the group to follow. Every step became more difficult than the last as the snow piled up around them—but at least it would obscure their footprints.

And even as the snow continued to fall and the wind howled around them, the group remained determined. They knew that they had to keep moving forward, no matter how hard the journey became. And with each step they took, they grew closer to their goal, fueled by the hope of what lay ahead.

The group emerged onto a new plateau. The weather was changing depending on how high or low they were on the mountain and if they were above or below the clouds. For now, the snowfall had stopped, and the sun shone down on them, providing a small amount of warmth. But with each step they took, they left behind an obvious trail of paw prints in the snow—a trail that would be all too easy for their pursuers to follow.

"The weather's not holding," Mufasa said. "If the white lions find our tracks, they'll follow them to Milele." He spotted the hornbill flying above and had an idea. "Zazu—only you can help us."

"Ermmmm, are we sure about that?" said Zazu. "No, I was actually thinking Rafiki looks pretty handy with the stick—it's almost like he's got five limbs, so . . ."

"Zazu, we need you. You can do this," Mufasa said.

"Yes, sir, you're right. I've got this," Zazu said.

With a determined look on his face, Zazu flew low to the ground, using his wings to swoop snow over the tracks of the rest of the group. Hard work and the bitter cold made his wings ache, but he refused to give up. Again and again, he covered the tracks, determined to leave no trace of their passage. The rest of the group watched in awe as Zazu's wings beat steadily, his body a blur of motion against the pristine white snow.

Finally, after what seemed like hours, Zazu landed on the ground, panting and shivering from the cold. But his efforts had paid off. Their tracks were now completely hidden, and they could continue on their journey without fear of being followed.

Mufasa, Taka, Sarabi, and Rafiki pressed on, emerging to find a glorious vista that looked out over cascading summits, so high above the ground that clouds floated past them. They were so entranced by the view that they almost didn't notice that Zazu had taken off to scout below.

∧∨∧∨∧

Farther down the mountain, the white lions approached the plateau, the two female hunters out front. They attempted to follow Mufasa's group's tracks, but the tracks stopped in the middle of the path, as if the gang had vanished into thin air.

"What's happening?" Kiros barked at them. "We can't keep stopping!"

"Somehow they've covered their tracks," Amara called back.

Kiros huffed, his ears twitching in anger. "In the snow? It's not possible!"

"Majesty," said Akua, "they could be anywhere on this mountain."

"Then find them!" Kiros shouted. "Find them now!"

The lions didn't notice a hornbill perched discreetly above them on a rocky ridge.

∧∨∧∨∧

Zazu took in the scene, then flew back to tell the group. They did deserve some good news after their miserable time traversing the snow. He soared up into the sky until he'd rejoined the group, arriving at Mufasa's feet with an awkward stumble.

"I have a report," Zazu said, nearly out of breath. "The white lions are completely lost. Well played, Mufasa."

"We did it," Mufasa said, looking squarely at Rafiki. Then he turned to Sarabi and Taka. "We did it."

Sarabi moved closer to Mufasa and nuzzled him.

"No, *you* did it," she emphasized. "Great thinking, Mufasa."

Taka looked onward, once more feeling like an outsider.

CHAPTER 21: BEFORE

In the middle of the night, Taka felt restless. He rose from his place and went toward the corner of the cave, grappling with his conflicting thoughts and emotions. Observing Sarabi's admiration for his brother had caused a pang of jealousy to stir within Taka's heart, and he questioned his own worth and desirability. Could he ever measure up to Mufasa's charisma and bravery?

As he settled in the corner, the ghost of his father, Obasi, appeared before him: "Taka, your name means 'spirit' because you are mine. Honor it, my son. Fulfill your destiny."

As his father faded away, Taka jolted awake. It had only been a dream.

When he examined the cave, though, Taka was shocked to discover that both Mufasa and Sarabi were missing. Mufasa often hunted at night, but that seemed odd for the lioness. Maybe she was nearby.

"Sarabi?" Taka called. He walked toward the opening of the cave to look out over the icy landscape, but he didn't see her—or anyone. "Sarabi?"

No. He was completely alone.

∧∨∧∨∧

Mufasa had woken from his sleep earlier that night. He'd left the cave, and he was hunting in a small moonlit clearing, silently waiting for his prey to emerge from its hiding place. Suddenly, Sarabi appeared behind him.

"Hidden in the shadows. Downwind, light afoot. You hunt like a girl, Mufasa," she said softly.

"We have to eat something before we take on that descent," he explained.

"Unfortunately, there's nothing to hunt up here,"
Sarabi said.

"See under that rock—there's a civet about to leave his
den." Mufasa gestured with his head.

Sarabi looked into the distance, and a sheet of white
snow and ice radiated back at her. There was no civet to
be found, she thought.

"Of course you can smell a civet hidden in the snow.
You . . . the lion who can do *anything*," she teased.

"What's that supposed to mean?" Mufasa quipped.

"It means, I see you, Mufasa. I've seen you from the
very beginning."

"I . . . I don't know what you're talking about," Mufasa
said, his voice tinged with a mix of curiosity and uncer-
tainty.

"Now that part I believe: you don't know what I'm
talking about. Because smart as you are, you have a way
of seeing everything but yourself."

The intensity between the two broke as a civet
squealed and belched. They both snapped toward the
sound.

"What is this?" said Mufasa. "What is this, Sarabi?"

"There's a civet in the snow, right where you said it would be," she said. "And you smelled the white lions on the wind. Which means you're the one who smelled the flowers on my fur."

"It was a lucky guess . . ." Mufasa said dismissively.

But Sarabi could see through his indifference. "You can smell the exact flower from my valley. . . ."

"No—that's not possible," Mufasa said.

"You saved me; held me, covered me in the stampede, comforted me—"

"No. It was Taka," Mufasa insisted.

"'I gotchu, I gotchu, Sarabi,'" she said, imitating Mufasa's voice in her ear as she'd lost consciousness during the stampede.

"I'm here to protect him," Mufasa said, somewhat revealing why he'd been untruthful.

"That was *you*," Sarabi asserted righteously.

"I was lost in the water—and he found me. My brother saved me," Mufasa said, his voice full of emotion.

"I sensed it from the beginning . . ." Sarabi said.

"His blood is the blood of the king!" Mufasa said.

"Mufasa!" Sarabi said, almost admonishing him.

"That is his destiny," Mufasa continued.

"No. His destiny was to save you. Now tell me it's you. . . ."

She already knew the truth but wanted to hear the words from Mufasa.

They didn't notice Taka staring at them, standing behind the trees. He watched as Mufasa moved closer and closer to Sarabi. The two confessed they had developed feelings for each other, and Taka turned away. He could no longer stand the embarrassment he had become.

He ran, wishing everything had been different. If he'd known that he would always live in the shadow of Mufasa's brilliance, maybe he wouldn't have ensured that Mufasa became his brother.

He sprang down the mountain, and everything blurred as he ran faster and faster. Once the terrain grew steeper, he hit an icy patch and lost his footing, falling, tumbling, and crashing through the trees, slamming into rocks on his way down the mountain.

Taka landed with a sharp thud in a sloped snow-covered clearing. Slowly he got to his feet and collected himself. Snow began to move in the distance—no, not snow. Kiros and the white lions approached from farther down the ridge. He could see them, but they could not see him.

The memory of his mother's words echoed in his head: *Taka, your moment of courage will come.*

Embracing the memory, Taka drew strength from the notion that courage resided within him, waiting to be awakened. He understood that true bravery was not the absence of fear, but the ability to confront and overcome it. And this was his chance.

He walked toward Kiros until he came into the white lion's line of sight. The stunned lions watched him approach.

Kiros looked over at his two grinning, salivating hunters, as they moved closer to the cowering Taka. Kiros couldn't help being amused at the lion's cowardice.

"There wasn't much to eat on this mountain until

now," Kiros said. "Tell me—how did you cover your tracks in the snow?"

Taka looked up at the empty sky, refusing to look Kiros in his blue eyes. "A bird helped us."

Kiros and the other lions burst into laughter.

"Lions getting help from a bird?" sneered Amara.

Taka bolstered himself and meekly stepped forward. "Just as I will help you."

"You will help us?" Akua repeated.

"You think we need help from a wounded coward?" said Kiros, and the group laughed more.

Taka stared at them sternly, and suddenly all fear vanished from his muscles.

"I may hold the blood of a king—but it was Mufasa who killed your son," he said. "It was Mufasa who trapped you up here—outsmarted you at every turn. Now I will lead you to him and Milele."

The white lions stopped laughing, their interest captured by Taka's new courage.

"Milele?" Kiros asks. "Milele is nothing but a dream. A vision sold to cubs."

"Oh, well, tell that to the monkey. He leads them to it," Taka said, making Kiros's ears perk up. "Look at you—a pack of starving wolves clinging to the side of a mountain! No tracks to follow—only one chance at revenge. Me!"

"Revenge?" Kiros asked, then paused. "What about your father?"

Taka went cold. "Because of Mufasa, I have no father."

"Yes. You lost a father. And I a son," Kiros said solemnly. "Taka, will you join us? Together, we can both have our revenge."

"It will be my pleasure . . ." Taka said. He lowered his head in deference and added: "King."

Kiros approached him—and, shockingly, laid his chin atop Taka's bowed head, almost affectionately. Kiros stepped back and paced for a moment, considering how he wanted to kill Mufasa in the most painful way. And nothing would be better than to let him know how his own brother betrayed him.

He turned to Taka, accepting him as his faithful companion. "Return to them. Let the monkey lead you. Scar the trees as you go, and we will follow. If a Milele is really out there, we will find it . . . and we will conquer it. And then," Kiros added with a growl that echoed across the land, "we will kill your brother."

Taka bristled at the assertion. "He's not my brother! He's a stray—and I will feed him to you. Trade an entire kingdom for his life."

Kiros merely smiled and chuckled to himself. "Mufasa . . . dies with the sun."

"Oh, what a sweet, sweet sound," Taka said.

No more of Mufasa outshining him in every field. Kiros and Taka made eye contact, sharing an unspoken agreement that they'd work together to bring Mufasa down.

∧∨∧∨∧

Taka returned to Mufasa and the rest of the group, oddly calm and filled with silent rage.

Mufasa turned to greet him, his face lit up with suspicion. "Taka—Taka, where have you been?"

Guilt traveled up Taka's throat, but he forced it back down. "Hunting. I couldn't find anything, but . . . I was never as good as you. Or my mother."

Taka hoped that Mufasa wouldn't ask too many more questions.

Mufasa sighed. "There's something I need to tell you."

Before he continued, Sarabi walked out of the cave they'd camped in and stood beside Mufasa.

"No," said Taka. "There's something I need to tell you. I need to thank you. You kept your word to Eshe and Obasi."

Mufasa looked at him with his brows raised as he whispered, "Taka . . ."

"You saved me, Mufasa," Taka said, his voice straining with emotion. "And I will never forget what you've done. My brother . . ."

Taka moved closer to Mufasa, but Zazu squawked, alerting the group to his presence.

"Oh, guys! I have found a way down just beyond those near peaks," the bird announced. He was covered in snow, half-frozen. When the others only stared, he added, "Was it something I said?"

Suddenly, the ground shook, causing a small avalanche on the far ridge.

"Rafiki," Mufasa started.

"Yes, Mufasa. I feel it," Rafiki said with a glimmer in his eyes.

The gang needed to get moving and start their descent. Taka let Sarabi and Mufasa move ahead of him, and as they left their spot, he stealthily swiped his sharp claw across a tree.

CHAPTER 22: NOW (INTERLUDE)

Timon, Pumbaa, and Kiara all stood up in the cave, anticipating the mandrill's next words.

"Okay, now I'm a hundred million percent sure who Taka is," said Pumbaa. "Just be honest: is it me?"

"In case you missed it, we're not featured in this. I think the civet has more screen time," Timon scoffed.

"Maybe they'll put us in the play," Pumbaa said, still optimistic.

"No, no, please don't mention the play again," Timon said. "I went to see it. I'm nothing but a giant sock puppet!"

"You went to see it and you didn't bring me?"

Timon and Pumbaa's banter faded into the background as Kiara walked away from them and toward Rafiki.

"Rafiki, Mufasa and Sarabi are in love," Kiara said.

Pumbaa darted closer at the mention of the word. "Ewww . . . love. That sounds gross. And not something I constantly think about and really want."

"What is Taka going to do to them?" Kiara asked, concern spreading across her face.

"Little one, Taka's heart was broken," Rafiki said. "And now his trap was set."

CHAPTER 23: BEFORE

First, Rafiki and Sarabi reached a clearing just below the clouds and stopped to look out in silent awe. Mufasa rushed ahead and caught a glimpse, too, and soon Taka joined them.

"Mufasa, do you see?" Rafiki asked.

"I don't believe it," Sarabi gasped.

The rising sun shone through dark clouds—a beacon in the storm.

"The other side of the light," Mufasa whispered, his eyes widening.

"Home," Sarabi responded right away.

"Home," Mufasa repeated.

"Milele," Rafiki corrected.

The word *Milele* resonated within Mufasa, carrying a profound meaning that he'd longed to discover ever since his parents had told him about this place. No longer were his eyes heavy from the long journey, or his paws sore. Relief radiated throughout his whole being.

Mufasa, Taka, Sarabi, Zazu, and Rafiki made their way into Milele, a paradise.

They walked underneath the belly of the blue sky and approached a pristine watering hole nestled in the heart of the savannah. Each creature's coat glowed in the warm golden light as they approached, their eyes fixed on the sparkling blue water. They reached the edge of the watering hole, and Mufasa sniffed the air, his whiskers twitching as he assessed the eerily empty surroundings, devoid of any other creatures.

His curiosity took over, and he began to play with the water. Sarabi grinned and joined him, and they splashed each other, sending droplets flying in all directions. But Rafiki had noticed something in the distance and began muttering to himself.

"I can't believe it!" said Mufasa. "We found it. We found Milele."

"Yes, you found it, Brother," Taka said. "You always do."

"He did indeed," Zazu said, flying down from above. "And Milele is amazing, but, well, this place being more or less a fairy tale and all, I flew around a bit to check things out. Well, if it is just us, seems like an awful waste of space."

"He has a point," Sarabi said. "Where is everyone? There should be others, right?"

"There should..." Mufasa began. He stopped to sniff the air, wondering why they were the only ones in this beautiful place. But it was almost like he could feel the eyes of creatures on him—even if he couldn't spot them just yet. Were they waiting to see what these new arrivals would do?

Then, suddenly, Rafiki began to shout and ran toward something he had been staring at in the distance: "*Ndoto yangu! Ndoto yangu! Ndoto yangu!*"

Mufasa, Taka, and Sarabi only observed him—until

they realized Rafiki was running toward an enormous tree and they decided to follow.

"What is it?" Mufasa called out.

Rafiki delicately touched the tree's giant roots and looked up through its long, intricate branches. He stood there in complete awe.

"I have seen this tree many times," Rafiki said. "And in each vision it was always empty."

"Empty?" Mufasa asked, coming up behind the mandrill. "But you came here to find your twin?"

"He was taken from me long ago. What I saw in my dream was a brother. Standing right here." Rafiki turned to Mufasa. "A friend. Family."

Rafiki reached out to touch Mufasa's face. "What I saw was you. The unseeable. I saw Mufasa!"

"Me?" Mufasa said.

"Yes! You! My brother!"

"Mufasa!" bellowed an unusual voice.

The group turned and saw an older giraffe staring intensely at them. Other animals—including a group of lionesses—appeared then, previously hidden in the valley.

"We know who you are," the giraffe said. The group stood frozen, looking up at the creature. "They are after you. You must leave here at once. It will never be safe with you here."

"It will never be safe anywhere unless we band together," said Mufasa.

A thunderous roar resounded from behind them. The gang and all of the animals looked up, frightened.

Mufasa spotted Kiros in the distance, leading his army of white lions over a ridge and into Milele.

Kiros sniffed the air, sensing Mufasa was near.

"Do not run!" Kiros shouted out to the animals. "You have nothing to fear! We are not here for you!"

The animals slowly backed away from Mufasa and his group.

"We have come for the last lions!" Kiros continued. "If there are lions here, show them to us and no harm will come to you. We have come for Mufasa!"

"Do not let him divide us!" said Mufasa.

"We have come for Mufasa," Kiros repeated.

Mufasa stiffened. He looked out at the kingdom of animals he had just been introduced to.

"Together we are many," he shouted. "As one, we are strong, stronger than any force imaginable. Let's stand together!"

"But why should we stand with you?" the wizened giraffe retorted. "We are not lions. This is your fight."

"Every being has a place in the Circle of Life," Mufasa said firmly. "My breath is your breath. Your fight is my fight."

Across the savannah, Kiros let out a savage roar, then laughed.

"It's no use, Mufasa," the white lion king said. "The circle . . . the circle is broken. From this moment on, everything the light touches belongs to me."

Enraged, Mufasa let out a roar—a deafening, emphatic sound of strength. "No! There will be no more running."

Kiros launched toward Mufasa, and the other white

lions quickly followed, running straight at them from across the ridge.

"Mufasa, what are you doing?" asked a panicked Sarabi.

"I'm going to fight," Mufasa said. His eyes shone with unwavering conviction. "I'm going to fight, and I'm going to show them that *they* can fight, too." He turned to the mandrill. "Rafiki?"

"Yes, my brother," Rafiki replied.

"When it's time," Mufasa said, "call them together."

Rafiki nodded. "*Nants ingoyanyama.*"

Kiros sniffed the air. "There are other lions here. Find them."

As the white lions dispersed, obeying the command, Sarabi approached Mufasa. She had a plan in mind—perhaps she could connect with those other lionesses who lived in Milele.

"Mufasa, you're not alone," she said. "It's my turn to go ask questions first." She turned to go but couldn't resist adding: "And just for the record, the bees worked. Even if they did cause a stampede."

Then Sarabi was off to enact her plan—but Taka still stood at Mufasa's side.

Kiros let out another roar, and Mufasa roared back. He would not hide anymore. He walked directly toward Kiros with Taka right behind him, until they were standing atop the entrances to several caves. He clenched his jaw, ready to fight for his life.

"This is where the hunt ends, Mufasa," Kiros said cheerfully. "Thanks to your brother."

Kiros nodded toward Taka, and confusion spread across Mufasa's face. Mufasa broke his gaze with Kiros to turn to his brother.

"Taka . . ." said Mufasa.

"He left a trail of scars for us to follow," continued Kiros. "Made a deal to save himself! Gave us this kingdom!"

"No, Taka, please—" Mufasa began as Taka avoided his gaze.

"Asked us to kill the stray!" Kiros went on.

Taka continued avoiding Mufasa's gaze. That alone

told Mufasa everything he needed to know. But still, he said, voice strained: "Tell me he's lying."

"I'm the son of a king, but Sarabi chose you," Taka snarled. "Just like Eshe—just like my own father! I saved you! And you betrayed me!"

"What have you done?" Mufasa snapped. "I'm your brother! Fight with me!"

Taka remained unmoved. "You stole my destiny. Now this is yours."

Taka crossed an invisible line in the dirt that separated the two sides and stood slightly behind Kiros. The once peaceful savannah was now a battlefield, with two powerful lions about to clash.

"He's one of us now," Kiros stated.

Mufasa stood alone, unable to tear his gaze away from Taka the traitor.

"My son's name was Shaju," said Kiros. "Shaju. All of this should have been his! And now I will rule it without mercy."

"You'll have to take it," said Mufasa.

Kiros's troops began to encircle him, but Kiros stepped forward, stopping them.

"This one . . . is mine," he announced.

Kiros lunged forward, swiping at Mufasa. Kiros's offensive move sent Mufasa back. Kiros only responded with quicker movements, demonstrating his pure strength and agility. He threw Mufasa across the rocks, and Mufasa struggled to get back up. He thought maybe he could recover and take on the other lion—but he made a snap decision to dash away, fleeing into a small ravine running along the hilltop ridge. Kiros chased him, nearly on his heels. Anxiety flushed through Mufasa's consciousness. Could this be his demise?

The remaining creatures of Milele fell into chaos. The herds of zebras and wildebeests, sensing the danger, stampeded away from the battle, their thundering hooves shaking the ground. Birds took to the sky, their wings flapping wildly as they tried to escape the conflict below. Gazelles darted across the plains, their slender legs carrying them as fast as they could go. And the pride of Milele lions was running as well, led by their matriarch.

Sarabi had found and followed the lionesses, running to the other side of the hilltop. She caught up to them and ran down to speak with the matriarch.

"We can't run forever," Sarabi said to the lioness. "We must stand our ground!"

"There's nothing we can do," the lioness said sadly. "They're too strong."

Sarabi noticed that the lioness was eyeing a small cub, watching from a ridge across the way. Sarabi seized this window of opportunity and pleaded, "Fight with us. Fight for your young."

The lioness saw a group of white lions crossing the grounds, in pursuit of that same young cub.

"Zuri? Zuri!" she shouted.

Zazu, flying above, eyed Zuri's tiny frame. Bolstering his courage, he landed in between her and the white lions.

"You've messed with the wrong hornbill!" Zazu declared.

The white lions advanced, clearly unimpressed with the bird.

"Lunch is served," said one of the hunters, Akua.

"Stay away!" Zazu said. "I'm double-jointed."

Zazu stood in a defensive fighting pose, and just as the white lions lifted their claws to strike . . .

A shoebill swooped in and grabbed up both Zazu and Zuri, one in each foot. He flew them to safety atop the summit of a steep hill, and Zazu whooped and cheered along the way.

Meanwhile, Mufasa found himself backed up against the edge of the ridge, Kiros's imposing form looming over him. His heart pounded as he desperately tried to keep his footing on the slippery surface beneath him. Suddenly, he lost his balance and slid down to a ledge below, barely managing to stop himself from plummeting farther.

As he looked up, he saw Kiros's fierce gaze fixed on him from above. Mufasa knew he was at a disadvantage, but he refused to give up without a fight. He noticed an opening into a cave below him, and he slipped inside.

Back at the rugged hill, Sarabi and the lioness raced up the side, their paws digging deep into the rocky terrain as they climbed higher and higher.

"Zuri," the lioness kept saying. "Zuri."

They arrived from the backside of the summit, coming face to face with Zuri and Zazu, who were waiting for them at the top. But then they spotted a group of white lions emerging from the hill below. Akua and Amara led the pack, their majestic forms silhouetted against the bright blue sky.

Mufasa stumbled into a large chamber deep in the cave, the only light filtering through small holes in the ceiling. As he moved cautiously through the chamber, he heard a strange noise.

"Mufasa," Kiros's voice echoed. "Mufasa."

He looked around frantically, trying to locate Kiros.

But as he gazed up into the light, he instead saw his brother peering down at him.

"Taka!" called Mufasa.

But his brother quickly disappeared from view.

"Taka," Mufasa repeated in despair. In the depths of his heart, Mufasa couldn't help questioning himself, wondering if there was anything he could have done differently to prevent this dire situation. He reflected on the choices he had made, the trust he had placed in his brother, and the painful realization that it had been a mistake.

With nowhere else to go, Mufasa walked farther into the cave's wide expanse. He had stopped to get his bearings when he heard footsteps from another passage of the cave.

Kiros appeared, flanked by two white lionesses. His eyes blazed with anger. "An ordinary lion. Common blood. Worthless. I . . . was *always* your destiny."

Kiros ran at Mufasa, sending the younger lion to the ground. As the white lion loomed over him, Mufasa took a deep breath, gathered his courage, and charged at Kiros with all his might. Miraculously, he managed to knock Kiros over. The lionesses, shocked that their leader had been bested, rushed to their king's aid. Mufasa took the opportunity to dart out of the same opening Kiros had entered through, determined to escape.

Mufasa's paws pounded against the rocky terrain as he darted through the caves, his heart beating furiously. He wasn't running away in fear but, rather, running toward a new challenge. His face was set in determination as he scaled the top of the cave and emerged onto the ground where he had previously faced off with Kiros.

With every leap and bound, Mufasa's muscles burned with exertion, but he pushed on, and as he ascended higher and higher, he could see the top of the hill looming in the distance, beckoning him forward.

He reached the highest point of the hilltop and paused for a moment to catch his breath. From his vantage point on the ledge, he could see out past the enormous tree and into the vast wilderness beyond. The view was breathtaking, and for a moment, Mufasa forgot about everything else as he basked in the beauty of the world around him.

Mufasa cast a swift glance behind him, catching sight of the white lions making their way over the distant hills. With fierce determination, he threw his head back and let out a powerful roar that echoed throughout the valley.

CHAPTER 24: BEFORE

The sound of Mufasa's roar reverberated through the Milele Valley and echoed back to him, filling him with a sense of power and purpose. Some creatures' heads turned at that sound.

As he gazed out over the vast expanse before him, he felt a sense of belonging, a connection to the land that was his home. He knew that he had a duty to protect it, and he would do whatever it took to keep it safe from those who would seek to harm it.

Mufasa roared again, louder. An insistent call resounded throughout Milele as all the animals raised their heads attentively. They followed the sound of Mufasa's roar, locating him atop the caves.

A silence seemed to settle among them as they saw the brave lion holding his ground. The herd stood still, motionless. They did not even dare to breathe, because in the middle of the herd, the white lions stalked through them, trying to finally capture the one they had been following for so many days. He did not have any place to escape to now.

Rafiki, among the herd, looked up at Mufasa as well. Mufasa could not see him, but Rafiki nodded up at him in recognition. Standing at the very top, with his body stretched, Mufasa looked regal, as though he could command the entirety of Milele if he wished to do so. But they had more immediate things to worry about.

Rafiki put his staff to the ground again as he walked on, shouting, "*Nants ingoyanyama bagithi. Nants ingoyanyama bagithi.*"

At the top of the caves, Kiros and a pair of white lions surrounded Mufasa. But the young lion remained rooted to his spot, at the highest point, a clear beacon for all below to see. As Kiros and the other white lions lunged toward him, he did not run away. He stood his ground and took them all on at once.

Meanwhile, below in the valley, Rafiki continued chanting, surrounded by a circle of towering baobab trees, their thick trunks and branches casting deep shadows on the ground. The soil beneath his feet felt soft and springy, and as he chanted, he could feel the power of the earth flowing through him. He closed his eyes, hoping that his chants would send Mufasa the energy he needed. And around him, the other animals watched the battle in awe.

Mufasa became entangled with the white lions. His adversaries took turns, scratching and clawing at him as Kiros stood a few feet away from the fight, hanging back to observe. Mufasa knew that whatever happened on this day, he would never be known as the lion who walked away, and he would never give them the satisfaction of calling him a coward because he did not stand his ground.

Mufasa summoned all of the energy he could muster and managed to get back onto his feet and spin himself over the cliff's edge. The white lions and Kiros stood back in amazement at Mufasa's sudden, dramatic move. They followed his parabola in the air and saw him land back inside the caves. But Kiros could smell another lion near him; he could almost feel it. He turned around and it was . . . Taka.

"Taka," said Kiros. "Let's finish this."

⌃⌄⌃⌄⌃

Back in the valley, the rest of the white lion army snaked through the throng of animals to hunt the Milele lions. The other animals, inspired by Rafiki's chanting, declared solidarity.

"We fight together," announced one buffalo.

And as the various herds encircled them, it became obvious that for once the white lions were outnumbered.

As Mufasa regained his bearings, looking up at the low ceiling he had fallen through, he heard the faint but noticeable sound of chanting drifting in. Bolstered, he examined his surroundings, trying to track where Kiros might attack from next. He had evaded the other two white lions and now waited for the real deal.

He found himself backed up near a sheet of water, a spray raining down from the cave roof—alone until Kiros leapt through the water, straight at him.

The two tussled, fighting until some bats flew toward Kiros, distracting him. The bats hurried out of the cave, straight past another lion watching from above: Taka, lurking in the shadows, looked down from a ledge.

He watched as Mufasa and Kiros went toe to toe. His breaths came out choppy now that he was unsure who would win this battle. And what would happen to him if Mufasa got rid of Kiros? Regardless of any regret he might feel, Taka had made his choice. It was unlikely he could ever win back the trust Mufasa had had in him, the trust he had betrayed. He had been willing to let Mufasa die at the hands of Kiros, a decision that weighed heavily on his conscience.

But the memories of their shared past, their laughter, and the camaraderie they had once enjoyed tugged at his conflicted emotions. As much as he wanted to bury those feelings, the undeniable brotherly connection remained, haunting him amid the turmoil of his choices.

⌄⌃⌄⌃

In the valley, Rafiki continued chanting, growing louder and louder in a staccato rhythm as he placed a hand on the ground, feeling the vibration.

Kiros stopped for a beat as the distant sound of Rafiki and the animals' call filled the cave, and he strained his ears to make out the words drifting down from the ceiling.

Mufasa gathered himself and went at Kiros swiftly, leaving the white lion lying in a heap.

Kiros wheezed from where he lay on the ground.

"You dare to challenge me!"

He got up with a groan and started swiping at Mufasa again and again. The continuous blows pushed Mufasa back, and the much larger lion had the advantage once more. Finally, Mufasa stopped struggling, unable to defend himself as Kiros moved in for the kill.

"You took my son, Shaju," said Kiros, "my future."

Mufasa remembered Eshe's smiling face as Kiros came at him one last time, feeling no regret for having killed Shaju to save her—and Mufasa could only watch as the white lion stood over him. Mufasa's mind then shifted to Sarabi. Memories of their shared moments, laughter, and kinship flooded his mind, intermingled with a deep sense of concern and worry for her safety. He also thought of Taka, because even though his brother had betrayed him, he still loved him.

Kiros raised a sharp claw high in the air. "Blood for blood!"

But just as Kiros brought his massive claw down, Taka leapt in front of his brother—and took the blow himself. He dropped to the ground, a new gash running down his face.

Taka growled low in his throat, struggling to stand up. "Please . . . don't kill him."

Kiros chortled. "I didn't kill him. You did."

Taka's heart clenched at his words. Kiros did not tell any lie, though. He had been the one to sell out his brother. He had let fear and jealousy guide his choices, disregarding the bond of brotherhood and loyalty that should have defined their relationship. The true weight of his betrayal pierced his heart, leaving him with an overwhelming sense of remorse.

Taka fully rose to his feet, blood staining the ground beneath him, and he saw confusion mingled with a flicker of gratitude in Mufasa's eyes.

He aligned himself with Mufasa—two against one now.

Kiros snickered, watching this play out, and then the brothers charged in—together.

∧∨∧∨∧

Back outside, the white lions reached the top of the slope, squaring off with the Milele pride.

Amara called out, "The last lions."

"Time for their extinction," Akua continued. "And we'll start with the youngest."

But suddenly, they felt the ground begin to shake. An earthquake traveled across Milele. A crack formed on the ground between the two prides and rapidly started to grow.

In the valley, Rafiki, with a hand to the ground, felt the shaking, too. Behind him, a white lion inched his way toward him. With his eyes closed, Rafiki stood helpless and alone. The white lion leapt toward him—only for a giant buffalo to slam into the lion's side, sending him back against the big tree.

On the hill, the crack grew between the two lion prides. As the white lions stepped forward, the muddy slope moved beneath their feet. They froze as they stood on the edge. The ground shook even more as a hint of fear crossed their eyes. They looked behind them, but they had no place to run.

Sarabi spoke up from the stable half of the hill, opposite the pride of white lions. "It's not too late to join us. Please. Come across."

She stepped aside to give them a clear path to safety— but the hunters turned back to their army.

"Attack!" cried Amara.

The lions moved to obey the command, but the massive hill gave way—and the earth dropped out beneath them. Rocks slid, and the white lions desperately tried to climb, but the ground kept disappearing. The hill dropped and transformed, and the mudslide carried the white lions down to the ground beneath, like a flood washing over them.

As the front side of that hill separated and fell to the ground, it formed a new rock structure—almost like a grand walkway that looked out over the expansive savannah.

The crumbled part of the rock structure landed with a crash, sending a massive tremor straight across the valley—all the way into the cave, where the brothers fought Kiros. Dust and debris rained down inside as Kiros pushed Taka back with a new blow. Kiros then turned and charged at Mufasa.

The floor gave way, and Mufasa and Kiros fell together into a giant pool of water below. Taka clung to the rim of the new hole, watching the other two lions disappear, the overwhelming rush of water engulfing their bodies in its chilling envelope.

Mufasa found himself sinking rapidly toward the bottom, unable to fight the pull of the watery depths. Panic welled up inside him. His eyes darted around as he desperately searched for an escape, but the weight of his fear froze him in place.

Kiros, on the other hand, swiftly kicked his powerful

limbs and propelled himself upward. A fleeting sense of relief washed over Kiros as he neared the water's surface, thinking he had won the race against their watery demise.

But then Mufasa heard a voice—Eshe, offering a sweet lull: *Mufasa, always be mindful of your rage. When your thoughts are clear, you cease to be prey.*

With newfound determination, Mufasa pushed through his panic and seized control of his sinking body.

Summoning every ounce of his remaining strength, Mufasa lunged toward Kiros, firmly gripping Kiros's hind leg with his claws. Ignoring his own dwindling air supply, Mufasa pulled Kiros back down into the depths, their bodies entwined in an underwater struggle.

Kiros started to panic as Mufasa dragged him lower and lower. Soon he was drifting beneath Mufasa, and he could only stare up at the younger lion as he fell into the tangled roots of a massive tree embedded at the bottom of the pool. No voice could come out of his mouth as he went deeper and deeper. As he felt his life slipping away, Kiros's sorrowful eyes met Mufasa's one last time.

The will to live took over, and Mufasa swam toward the surface, his muscles burning with exertion. Panic teemed through his body as he desperately searched for any sign of aid. If no one came to help him—he was sure to join Kiros beneath the waves, teetering on the brink of survival.

CHAPTER 25: BEFORE

As Mufasa approached the water's surface, his eyes locked with Taka's. His brother was still here. On instinct, and despite Taka's wavering loyalties, Mufasa frantically swam up to his brother. Taka reached down with sharp claws . . . and, mercifully, pulled his brother out of the water.

Gasping for breath and covered in water, the two brothers stumbled back into the safety of the cave. They stood there, their wet fur clinging to their bodies, as the weight of their actions settled upon them.

Sarabi, Rafiki, and Zazu rushed over from inside the

cave while Mufasa exhaled deeply, relieved to see his friends safe.

"Mufasa!" Sarabi said.

After sharing one last look with his brother, Taka, overwhelmed by shame and regret, swiftly retreated into the darkness, leaving Mufasa behind. He disappeared from sight, his presence marked only by the fading echoes of his footsteps. Sensing that Taka needed time to himself, Mufasa let him go.

Mufasa walked out of the cave with Sarabi at his side and found thousands of animals gathered in the valley below: herds of rhinos, baboons, hippos, giraffes, and other animals, big and small, standing together. As they approached the big tree, Rafiki appeared from the throng and gestured at the herds. Together, the trio descended farther into the valley.

When Mufasa walked past the animals, their voices rang out across Milele: "The king of Milele! The king! The king of Milele!"

Mufasa looked around the valley, his brows bunched up. "King? No. No, I'm not your king."

The animals remained adamant. "The king!"

"Raise your heads!" said Mufasa. "I'm just . . . No more kings. We are all one. Please. Please. Raise your heads."

But the animals ignored him and bowed even lower.

Rafiki stepped forward. "Mufasa, the king of Milele!"

"No, Rafiki, I'm not the king. I have no royal blood," Mufasa said.

"Don't you see, my brother—it is not what you *were*. It is what you have . . . *become*. The king of Milele!"

Mufasa wanted to protest more. Surely, Rafiki's excitement over Kiros and the white lions' defeat had made him exaggerate this moment's importance.

But then a familiar voice interrupted Mufasa's thought. His name rang out through the savannah, and his impulse was to start running toward it. Could it really be?

"Mother!" Mufasa said, his voice almost cracking.

It had been a long time since Afia had heard her son's voice, but she could recognize it out of thousands without a doubt. Coming from opposite ends of the savannah, Mufasa and Afia pushed their way through the throng of animals. The mother and son continued calling for each other, fueled by their unbreakable bond, their voices getting closer and closer. They finally reached each other and stood there with an audience surrounding them.

"Mufasa . . ." said Afia. "But how can it be? I had a son named Mufasa. Taken from me by a great flood."

"Mother!" Mufasa choked out.

The older lioness looked at him affectionately. "I never stopped hoping, believing, my son." Mufasa felt a sense of peace wash over him as he embraced Afia, holding her close to him. "Oh, Mufasa . . ."

Mufasa looked behind her for another figure. "Where is Father?"

Afia leaned in to whisper, "He lives in you now. He lives in you. I always dreamed we'd be together again. And I knew we would be in Milele. My son."

He felt his father's presence within him, guiding him and giving him strength. As they stood there, surrounded by the flatland of the Milele Valley and the herds of animals that roamed free, they knew that they were exactly where they were meant to be.

As Mufasa continued to take this in, Taka appeared before him.

He bowed his head and said, "Mufasa, please forgive me."

Mufasa, momentarily stunned, approached Taka with caution. Mufasa's gaze never wavered, scrutinizing Taka's every movement, searching for signs of sincerity and change.

Zazu flapped his wings. "You must banish him, sire."

The tides of emotions surged within Mufasa's heart. Hurt, betrayal, and longing for reconciliation clashed within him. He knew that forgiveness was a complicated and delicate process, one that required genuine remorse and a commitment to change. Yet the bond of brotherhood, no matter how fractured, still flickered deep within him.

"As long as I'm king," said Mufasa, "my brother will have a place here."

Taka's head bowed even lower. "Brother . . . I'm so sorry."

Mufasa walked closer to him. "But I won't ever say your name again. I can't. I won't."

"Then call me Scar," said Taka—a clear reference to the gash down his face. "So I will never forget what I've done."

Mufasa remained silent before muttering, "Scar."

Scar slowly bowed his head again. "Your Majesty."

The newly named Scar hurried away toward the base of the large rock structure. He was acutely aware of the journey he needed to undertake to fully earn Mufasa's forgiveness. However, Mufasa had not turned him away, and a new sense of possibility fueled renewed determination within him.

Sarabi stepped forward to greet Mufasa. "Welcome home, Your Majesty."

They both stood beneath the tip of the plinth. Mufasa looked up at it—majestic and humbling.

Rafiki motioned with his staff toward the peak. "It's your time, Mufasa."

Mufasa walked up to the summit, and animals big and small surrounded the base of what would soon become known as Pride Rock. Though his brother had truly broken his heart, he still had Rafiki, Sarabi, and even his mother at his side. They would be his pillars of support, reminding him that he was not alone on his journey. He was ready to be the king.

As rays of light streamed down on him, he surveyed the land that was now his kingdom. And he let out a triumphant roar that echoed across the Pride Lands, signifying that he was set to reign as the lion king for many years to come.

CHAPTER 26: NOW (EPILOGUE)

Kiara could picture the scene before her, as if it were a living tapestry unfurling in her imagination. She could almost see her grandfather, Mufasa, standing atop Pride Rock, a majestic figure silhouetted against the backdrop of the setting sun. The golden hues of the evening sky bathed him in a regal glow, accentuating his noble presence.

In her mind's eye, Kiara envisioned the pride gathered below, their eyes uplifted in reverence and anticipation. They looked to Mufasa, their leader, with trust and admiration, knowing that he possessed the strength and wisdom to guide them through any challenge.

Mufasa stood tall, his mane flowing in the gentle breeze, as he surveyed the land before him. His gaze encompassed the vastness of the Pride Lands, the beauty of its diverse landscapes, and the harmony of its inhabitants.

"Don't you see, Kiara?" Rafiki said. "He lives in you. He lives in you."

Kiara could almost feel the unspoken connection between generations, a bond forged not only by blood but by shared love for their homeland. Kiara let out a loud, triumphant roar, too, wanting to be just like Mufasa. Her fears about her own family faded away, and as the sun broke through the clouds, she could sense the ghost of her grandfather. Because he did live in her.

Still, Kiara couldn't help feeling a twinge of sadness. "I don't want him to go, Rafiki."

Rafiki shook his head. "It does not end, little one—it continues with you. Look out there. One day a female will rule it all."

Kiara huffed. "But there's no such thing as a female lion king."

Rafiki stepped forward. "Remember who you are, Kiara. You will choose what you will be."

∧∨∧∨

The storm finally ended and the sun shone through. Spotting her father and the others returning from their journey, Kiara bounded out of the cave and down to the savannah.

"Dad!" she shouted. "Dad!"

"Kiara!" Simba replied. "Kiara . . ."

She jumped up and held her father tight as she asked, "Dad, where's Mom?"

Simba patted her on the head. "Well, love, there's something you need to know."

Kiara stumbled back, fearing the worst. "What? Did something happen to Mom?"

"I'm right here." Nala's voice emerged from behind Simba. "And I'm fine."

Kiara's eyes widened as they fell on her mom, and she rushed toward her. "Where were you?"

As Nala moved aside, Kiara's eyes landed on a small cub moving between Nala's legs. The sight instantly melted Kiara's heart, and a surge of affection washed over her. She smiled and crouched down to examine the furry little creature.

"Kiara," Nala said gently, "this is your new brother."

"Brother!" she repeated. Kiara's eyes widened before she pounced over to him. "I have a brother?"

Her baby brother looked scared, unsure of the world around him. Kiara got even closer, nuzzling the frightened cub, offering a warm, welcoming smile.

"Hi, there," she said. "I'm Kiara—and I will take care of you forever, little one. Let me tell you a story—a story of a great king."

Simba and Nala exchanged looks, smiling proudly down at their daughter and son cuddled together, knowing that everything would turn out all right.

The Circle of Life continued.